Leashed

June Whyte

A Kat McKinley Greyhound Mystery
Book 4

White City

Press

Books by June Whyte

Sex on Tuesdays

THE GUMSHOE CHICK MYSTERY SERIES

Gone to the Dogs
For the Love of Dogs
Doggone It!

VETS 2U MYSTERY SERIES

Murder at Kangaroo Downs
Death at Dingo Creek
Homicide at Emu Lodge

KAT MCKINLEY GREYHOUND MYSTERIES

Chasing Can Be Murder
Muzzled
Hounded
Leashed

CHIANA RYAN CHILDREN'S MYSTERIES

The Case of the Disappearing Corpse
The Case of the Missing Dinosaur Egg
www.amazon.com/author/junewhytebooks

Leashed

June Whyte

This edition published by White City Press
An imprint of Misti Media LLC
https://www.mistimedia.com
Available in both Paperback and eBook Editions
1 2 3 4 5 6 7 8 9 10
Text Copyright © June Whyte 2024
Cover Copyright © 2024 by White City Press
Paperback ISBN: 9781963479430
eBook ISBN: 9781963479287

For my daughter, Melissa who's always there for me with a chat or cuddles or chocolate – or sometimes all three.

1

IF THE STENCH OF ROTTING FOOD DIDN'T KILL ME, my fiancé, Benjamin Taylor, would.

"Can you see it, Kat?" Tanya Ashton, my BFF, was currently holding one of my ankles in a death grip to prevent me from disappearing head first into the unthinkable depths of a commercial sized dumpster. She dug her talons more tightly into my flesh as she spoke.

"No, not yet!"

"Well look harder. My race is coming up in a minute." Jules Cassidy, a fellow greyhound-trainer and one of my soon-to-be bridesmaids, had her equally claw-like fingers wrapped around my other ankle.

"Sorry, Jules, but the stink in here's putting me off. I can't breathe. It's like being face down in the loo." I let out a cramped sigh. Couldn't risk a deep open-mouthed one. "A loo that hasn't been flushed for a month."

If only I'd taken the time to visit a jeweler after Ben went down on one knee and proposed to me six months ago. A size too big, my engagement ring dropped on the table while Tanya, Jules, and I were gorging on hot meat pies drowned in tomato sauce in the cafeteria at the Gawler dog-track. Somehow, in my hurry to get to the kennel-house and rug-up Big Mistake for the third race of the day, I must have gathered the ring with the remains of the pies and the brown paper bags, and ditched everything in the cafeteria's rubbish bin before rushing off to the kennel-house. It wasn't until after the race while punching the air in excitement at Lofty's ten length win that I discovered my engagement ring was missing. And by the time Tanya, Jules, and I hot-footed it back to the cafeteria to rescue my ring, the waste-bin had been emptied into the large dumpster at the rear of the track.

Which was the not-so-short-version of why, at one o'clock on a Tuesday afternoon, four days before I was due to marry the love of my life, I was upside down, sorting through nose-smarting garbage, inside a dumpster at the back of the Gawler dog-track.

"You'll never find your ring in amongst all that crap," said Jules and I could practically hear the eye-roll that went with her comment. "It'll be buried by now."

"Don't be such a glass-half-full."

"Sorry, hon. My mind's on the next race. You know I'd jump in there and help you in a heartbeat, but it's almost time to grab Cross Keys from the kennel house."

I grunted in reply.

"Feel awful though, leaving you here, head first in garbage."

"Thass okay." Talking while holding my breath to negate foul smells wasn't proving to be an easy option. As for Jules jumping in the dumpster to help me, I believed her. If Cross Keys was in a later race, she'd be in here ninja-style. She'd take a flying leap, land like a virile stag, knees bent, back straight, head high, and all without mussing up one hair on her head. Then, with her 20/20 vision, she'd spot my ring before I could finish saying, 'watch out for those soggy fish heads.' At 25, Jules played State netball, excelled at kick-boxing, climbed mountains for relaxation and had represented her age group in target shooting competitions in every state of Australia. Quite a handy friend to have onside.

"Hey, I'm being paged," Jules's grip on my ankle loosened, bringing me back to the present with a gasp. "Gotta go."

"Jules!" Tanya's nails hooked into my flesh. "Don't let go until I get a better grip or I'll lose her."

"Sorry, they're calling for me."

Abruptly, one set of hands disengaged from my left ankle leaving me upside down, lopsided, and arms scrabbling in the air for purchase.

"Kat! I can't hang on!" Tanya's sharp nails gouged deep painful runnels in my skin as her fingers began their inexorable slide. "I'm losing my grip!"

And with that, I landed with a smothered *oomph*, face first in something squishy and slimy that smelt and tasted a lot like fly-blown sausage rolls. Face contorted, I sucked air in through my teeth and quickly spat it out again. Dumpster air smelled worse than my sister's boyfriend's socks which he only changed when they stood up and barked at him.

"You okay?"

"No, I'm dying in here."

"Well, find your ring and get out."

I pushed myself into a kneeling position, tried not to think of what I was actually kneeling in, wiped something–not sure what and didn't want to know–out of my eyes, and took a shallow breath. I figured breathing deeply inside a partly-closed dumpster must surely be detrimental to one's health. "Tanya, please, you've gotta come in here and help me. Two sets of eyes are always better than one…"

I could hear Tanya's snort through the thickness of the bin. "Climb in there? With you? And get covered in dumpster slime? Geez, I'd rather play chicken with the cars on a busy highway. Anyway," she said as though there was no way of getting around her final justification. "I only bought this top yesterday."

"Well take it off then." Problem solved. "Please, Tan. I have to find my engagement ring. Otherwise Ben will be hurt. He'll think I don't care."

"Damn, now you're going to start bringing up the sob stuff." She let out a sigh of the doomed. "Okay, okay. I'll see if I can climb–" There was a soft gasp. "Shhh! Don't make a sound. Someone's coming. Oh! Uh! It's Toby Pearson."

That'd be right. Toby Pearson, down from Mt. Gambier for the day with his racing team, had to pass by right at this moment. I sighed. Surely nothing could be more embarrassing than to be found by a fellow trainer scrabbling around inside a garbage bin while waiting for the next race. I stared at a messy yellow food splatter on the far wall. Reminded me of a misshapen banana or maybe a deformed penis.

"Hi Toby, how's it going?"

"Oh, g'day, Tanya. Great win by Kat's dog in the last race. Couldn't back him though – price far too short." He hesitated. "Where *is* Kat? Collecting her winnings?"

"Um…I guess she's hanging around somewhere."

Not any longer…

"Actually, I'm glad I caught you on your own." Uh! Oh! Sounded like Toby was settling in for a nice long private chat. "It's Jan's and my six-week wedding anniversary next Saturday and I thought while I was down here I might buy something special from your shop, you-know, something kinky for me and the little wife to, sort of, play around with in the bedroom on Saturday night." Evidently a little embarrassed, Toby was gabbling at warp speed. Probably trying to get everything in before I came back from collecting my mythical winnings. "Um… so… anything you can suggest?"

"As a matter of fact, I can recommend some sexy new dress-ups that arrived at our shop yesterday," said Tanya, who worked at *The Luv Bug*, a wildly colorful and modern 'Adult' shop in the little town of Virginia. "Dress-ups are all the rage at the moment. And you know what, Toby? You'd look fiendishly edible in the latest schoolboy outfit and ..."

I tuned out. This could take a while. Tanya had no qualms when it came to selling sex enhancers and once she began her sales spiel she usually lost track of time. Looked like I was back to using only *one* set of eyes to find my ring.

While Tanya and Toby continued to discuss the pros and cons of the *The Luv Bug's* new crotchless dress-ups, I studied the kitchen slops, the stained race books, the half-eaten sweets, the dirty nappies, the cigarette butts – and my heart sank. Who was I kidding? The only way I'd find my ring was to come clean and contact the manager of Gregor's Skips. Then I'd need to plead, cajole and likely pay as much as the ring was worth for a couple of their pick-up guys to dump the contents of the bin in a pile and help me sift through the detritus.

Ready to run up the white flag and accept Ben's frustrated, I-told-you-so's, I glanced across to the far corner of the bin. And that's when I spotted what looked like the remains of our pies, plus the screwed up brown paper bags we'd thrown away. All tucked up beside a pile of discarded betting tickets.

Maybe this was my lucky day after all.

On hands and knees, inch by inch, I headed toward the remains of our lunch. It's not like you're skimming across the top when you crawl over garbage. Far from it. With every movement, I sunk deeper and deeper into the trash. A lot like crawling through thick oozing mud or wet cement.

Half way across, I stopped for a breather, shook a half-eaten lollypop out of my hair, and checked how much further to go. Another twelve or fifteen inches and I'd be able to reach out and check through those paper bags.

Feeling more optimistic, I set off again on what felt like a journey of a thousand miles. Ever-so-slowly...one hand in front of the other...knees dragging along behind...not stopping again until my right palm pressed down on what felt like...

Soft. Cold. Flesh.

Heart frozen in mid-beat, I snuck a sideways glance from the corner of one eye. And almost toppled backwards in my haste to snatch my hand away.

Was that a face?

In the claustrophobic atmosphere of the dumpster, with the familiar sound of the track's race broadcaster calling the fourth race on the program, I forced myself to take another look. Oh God, I knew that face. It was…no, it couldn't be. Balancing on both knees and one hand, I brushed the remains of stinking fish away from the eyes and nose and the upper half of the woman's body. And blinked. Puzzled. Why would greyhound racing's biggest slut, Mary Parker, be lying curled up inside a dumpster? Had she passed out, drunk? Was she asleep?

But what made me madder than a bee in a bottle – my engagement ring was balanced precariously on the woman's botoxed forehead. Bitch. She'd tried to pinch my fiancé and now she'd stolen my engagement ring. I frowned as Mary's unnatural stillness slowly filtered its way through my angry, fogged-up senses. This picture wasn't right. No way would Miss Sex-on-a-Stick be found sleeping in a dumpster – especially on her own. My eyes travelled from her thickly made-up face, to her scrawny forty-year old neck, to her recently completed way-out-there breast-implants, and came to a juddering halt.

Nooooo! Not again!

Right in the center of Mary Parker's greatly-enhanced chest was a jagged bullet hole. A hole that even the Plastic Surgeon to the Stars had no hope of fixing.

Oh God. Fighting the need to puke, to faint, to knock myself out on the side of the dumpster in the hope I'd wake up in the quiet sanctuary of my bedroom, my over-taxed brain fizzed and blew a fuse. While my heart, also scrabbling to escape, leapt into my throat and caused an instant blockage. A blockage that refused to allow a horrified scream to emerge from my mouth as anything but a stifled sob.

Then, gasping, gurgling and choking on my own spit, I snatched my engagement ring from the dead woman's forehead and morphed into Spiderwoman. I clambered up and over the walls of the metal dumpster – a fete my normal self would never manage in a million years – and ended up in a splattered heap on the ground at Tanya's feet.

Tanya screamed and leaped backwards. "What the–"

"It's…its…Mary Parker!" I gulped down a quick breath and swallowed a brick-sized lump in my throat in an effort to calm my over-jazzed-up heartbeat. "She's inside the dumpster."

"What's Mary doing in the dumpster?

"She's dead!"

Tanya opened her mouth to speak but no words came out.

"As dead as the flowers in your front garden," I reiterated before pushing myself up from the ground and checking to see if anyone was within hearing distance. Thankfully, Tony had finished his 'adult' conversation and moved on.

Mouth still open, Tanya blinked at me a couple more times before managing to find her voice. Her anxious eyes seemed to be pleading with me to turn this conversation into a tasteless joke. "Kat, you're not making a lot of sense. Why's Mary in the dumpster? And are you sure she's dead?"

"I don't know *why* she's in there, do I? And if she's not dead after taking a bullet to the heart she must be one of those mythical Immortal Lords that Gena Showalters writes about." I ran a hand through the slime in my hair and realized tears were not far away. "Guess I should ring the police and report it, hey?"

Tanya closed her eyes and her shoulders slumped. "Geez, Kat, what is it with you? Why do you keep finding dead bodies?"

"Hey, it's not that I go looking…"

"I know, I know. Sorry, I'm stressing here. And what's worse, there's no way I can get stuck into something alcoholic to make it all better. I have to drive home." Tanya looked longingly in the direction of the race-track bar. Normally only a social drinker, she always turned into a legless drunk whenever a dead body showed up. "Look, Kat, I've been thinking…"

"And?" I stared at her like she was the Sage of the Universe. The Dalia Lama's twin sister. Socrates Incarnate. My brain was complete mush, so whatever Tanya could come up with was my only hope.

"I think we should just walk away and let someone else find Mary's body."

"Whaat?"

"Think about it. Didn't you have an all-out row with the woman about the way she was draping herself over Ben at Angle Park dog-track last night? A quarrel that everyone heard – *and* where a racing steward had to intervene?"

"Yes, but–"

"And didn't you threaten to carve the word, slut, across her fake boobs if she tried to kiss your man one more time?"

"Um…yeah, but I didn't say anything about *shooting* her."

"And, the Big One. The one you should *really* take a few moments to reflect on. You, Kat McKinley, are due to be married in four days' time and Ben, your future husband, will *not* be happy if he has to say, 'I do', through the bars of a jail cell."

I let out a groan and buried my face in my hands. Now that one *did* make sense.

2

AN HOUR AND A HALF LATER, while teaching a couple of recently retired greyhounds the consequences of galloping on slippery floors, I heard a car pull up outside the granny flat we'd recently built to assist in turning switched-on racing dogs into couch-potatoes.

It was Detective Inspector Adams from the Elizabeth Police Precinct.

"Careful there. Watch where you're running big fella." The DI, looking his usual scruffy, down-at-heel self, stood just inside the doorway protecting his vitals with both hands as an out-of-control 35kg brindle greyhound surfed down the passageway and crashed into him.

The dog shook his head and grinned up at the Detective Inspector as if to say: *'Hey, that was fun! Wanna do it again?'*

"Sorry about Rufus," I said, hurrying over to sort dog parts from man parts. "He's still on his L plates. He thinks polished floors are made specifically for him to slide on. He also regularly smashes his nose on the glass doors leading outside because he can't remember they're for looking through – not galloping through." I gently ruffled Rufus's ears and then sent him into the lounge room, to rest up on the couch or on one of the pretty pink dog-beds set up for the GAP greyhounds to use. "He's only been here for a week. He'll learn."

I knew why DI Adams was here. Hell, I'd expected him, plus a couple of police cars with their sirens yowling, well before this. Contrary to Tanya's advice, I'd reported finding Mary Parker's body to the Chief Steward at the track, immediately before collecting the two dogs I'd raced that day and sneaking off home.

"Why did you leave the scene of a crime before the police arrived, Kat? You know better than that."

No 'hello' or 'nice day' just straight into the hard stuff.

"I needed a shower," I told him staring fixedly at the polished wooden floor. "I stunk of dog's poop, rotten fish and vomit."

What I didn't tell him was that I'd stood under the near-boiling water for half an hour in a vain attempt to wash away the cooties from Mary Parker's dead body. And the all-encompassing fear.

"Huh." Adams grunted, running a hand through his mop of uncombed, always-overdue-for-cutting, dark hair. "You need a better excuse than that. I could cuff you right now, pile you into the back seat of my car and then throw you into an empty cell at the police station and no one would blink an eye."

I turned my back on him to reach into the cupboard for two large mugs. "Well, why aren't you?"

He dragged out a chair and collapsed, legs stretched out, shoulders slumped. "God, I'm tired. Just came from a god-awful car crash where three little kids' broken bodies had to be cut out of a vehicle while their father, high on ice and doing 80ks over the speed limit, escaped with little more than a scratch." He shook his head and unconsciously reached down to stroke a passing Rufus who'd decided there was no food in the 'doggy lounge' but movement in the kitchen might mean treats. "Hard to fathom God's reasoning sometimes."

"Personally, I don't know how you keep doing your job, day in day out, without losing it. I'd end up banging my head against a brick wall."

"As they say – someone's gotta do it."

Poor guy looked beat. Okay, he always looked as though he'd slept in his clothes and lost his hair brush a year ago and hadn't got around to buying a new one, but today the lines on his face were deeper and the whites of his eyes red. "How about I add an inch of brandy to your coffee?"

"Don't tempt me."

"So…you haven't told me why you're not producing those handcuffs," I said spooning coffee into the mugs and praying I wasn't provoking him into action.

"Still might. Anyway, what is it with you and dead bodies? You're always stumbling over them–or in this case–sharing a dumpster with one." He rummaged in a pocket of his out-of-shape trench coat, pulled out a battered cigarette, sniffed it and placed it on the table in front of him. To look at? To light up if his will-power wasn't strong enough to resist? He let out a sigh. "Are you ready for me to take your statement?"

"Ask away."

He dragged a coffee stained notebook from one pocket, searched through several more pockets until he finally came up with a biro. "Now, I was told by several witnesses that you had an argument with the deceased at the track last night and threatened to, I'm quoting here, 'carve *slut* across her fake boobs'. Is that correct?'"

I sniffed. "She said Ben could do much better than me. That *she* knew how to give him real sexual pleasure. She even said that Ben constantly complained about how pathetic I was in bed." I waved an arm in the air. Rufus, thinking I was ordering him back to the lounge, grabbed an empty biscuit packet and trotted off with it in his mouth. "Naturally, I wanted to punch her lights out. Wouldn't you?"

"You actually believed Ben would say *that*?"

I rubbed my eyes, suddenly feeling as weary as the Detective Inspector. Also, rather small and stupid. Why had I allowed someone as manipulative as Mary make me feel inferior? Of course Ben wouldn't say those things. He barely acknowledged the woman when she tried to insert herself between us. "Guess not." I took a breath. "It's just that she always gets me…got me…so riled up. So…self-doubting…insecure of Ben's love. Every time she saw me with Ben she'd pucker up those fire-engine red lips, shove her enormous boobs in his face and drape herself all over him." I shrugged one shoulder. "I dunno…I guess the wedding-nerves got to me at the track last night and I just lost it when she started on me."

Eyes never leaving mine, he said, "So, did you lose it completely later on and kill Mary Parker?"

I shook my head. "Often felt like it, but, no, I didn't."

"Any idea who would have a reason to kill her?"

"A reason to kill her?" I distractedly watched Rufus drop his empty biscuit packet on the carpet and steal a stuffed green crocodile toy from one of the other dogs. "Too many to list, I'm afraid. Every married woman, girlfriend or fiancé in the greyhound industry would be more than happy for Mary to disappear. She was what you'd call, a serial man-stealer."

A tinge of a smile tugged at his lips. "In that case maybe I can leave the handcuffs in my pocket. At least until after your wedding."

I handed him a strong coffee, black, no sugar, with a large dollop of brandy added – figuring what he didn't see he couldn't be held responsible for–and sat down on the other side of the table.

"Thanks. I think."

"You know if we find a gun in your possession matching the gun Mary Parker was killed with, all bets are off."

"Feel free to search. I don't own a gun. Never have done. My weapons of choice are a can of hair-spray to the eyes a knuckle-duster to the nose and a knee in the what-nots. You'll find the hairspray and the knuckle duster inside my tote-bag. As for my knee, it's always wide-awake."

"Good to know." He took a sip of his coffee, rolled it around in his mouth for a moment before swallowing. "However, a team of policemen with a warrant will be here in around fifteen minutes to search your premises."

"Entertainment for the neighbors? How exciting. The Keystone Cops rolling up to converge on my house and kennels? Can't wait."

"Sorry, one of the DCI's conditions. Only way he'd allow me to take your statement here instead of at the station. But don't worry. The boys won't disturb you unduly." He took another sip of his coffee and his shoulders began to relax. "Now, next question. Did you see anyone in the area when you and your friends rocked up, ready to launch your little dumpster exploration today?"

"If we'd seen anyone hanging around, do you really think I'd embarrass myself by going ahead with the plan?"

"Okay, now we come to the inexplicable. Why *were* you crawling around inside a dumpster full of garbage?"

"The caterers accidently threw my engagement ring in there and you can imagine what Ben would say if he found out. So, naturally, I decided to look for the ring myself."

He spluttered coffee down his already egg-stained tie. "How did you expect to find a ring in amongst all that garbage?"

"Funnily enough, I did. It was perched on Mary Parker's forehead."

"Oh no, please, don't tell me you removed vital evidence from a crime-scene." He closed his eyes and I could hear him counting to ten under his breath.

"Um…has anyone thought to search the bin for the murder weapon?" I asked, eager to steer DI Adams away from thoughts of the vital evidence which was now back on my finger, thoroughly and meticulously sterilized. "It could save your guys a lot of wasted time searching for a non-existent gun in my house."

The DI let out a frustrated sigh before opening his eyes. "Yes, the manager of Gregors' Skips gave the all-clear for one of my men to hitch the mobile bin to a police car and tow it to the station. Several constables armed with face masks are sifting through the waste as we speak."

I sniffed. "So, as it turns out, I didn't need to get into that stinking dumpster after all. I could have left it to the police to find my ring." I thought it through a bit more. "And then it wouldn't have been me who found Mary's body?"

"Bit convoluted, but I guess you're right. Then again, someone had to find the poor woman's body." The Detective Inspector sighed. I'd never seen him look so worn-out. Maybe he had problems at home as well as at work.

Opting to make the DI another medicinal coffee, I pushed my chair back from the table and while collecting the empty cups, noticed Petunia, a small black and white greyhound with the sweetest personality, tiptoe in from the lounge. I smiled at her. It was as though the dog sensed the man's unhappiness. She went straight to the DI, rested her head on his lap and asked with her eyes for a pat.

"Petunia thinks you'd make a good Dad," I said, smothering a grin when the policeman's taut face relaxed into a smile as he gently rubbed one large hand over the dog's head. "Why don't you adopt her? She'd be no trouble. And think of all that unconditional love waiting at home for you when you walk through the door after a bad day at work."

He lifted one eyebrow and gave me a mock scowl as I placed his refilled coffee mug in front of him. "Nice try, Katrina, but not going to happen. Dogs don't need owners who live by my ridiculous work-schedule." Coffee in hand, he looked around. "Anyway, what's with this new building and the doggy play area outside? Is this where you're going to stash Ben when you two get married?"

"Only when he's in the dog-house." I laughed and watched the DI lean back in the chair and close his eyes. The hijacked coffee was doing its job. "No, this little house was built for the GAP dogs."

"GAP dogs?"

"Dogs in the Greyhound Adoption Program. While Ben immerses himself in the racing side of things, I'm going to foster retirees. Like this lot here. I'll socialize them over a six-week period and then rehome them as forever pets with suitable owners."

"Won't you miss full-time training?"

"Not really. I'll still train a few dogs but I'm looking forward to working with the retired pooches. They're a lot of fun."

"And there's always a granny-flat to hide in when your crazy sister and her hippie friends come visiting." Laughing, the DI plucked his ringing phone from his back pocket and jammed it to his ear. "DI Adams."

After listening for a few minutes, he swallowed the last of his coffee, returned the solitary cigarette to his pocket, almost reverently, and clambered to his feet. "Guess you're off the hook–for the moment."

"They found the murder weapon in the dumpster?"

He gave a sharp nod and headed for the front door. "But don't even think about leaving town without informing me first. 'Cos if your finger prints match those on the murder weapon, I'll be back to measure you up for handcuffs quicker than you can sew on a button."

"I don't do buttons," I told him. "When a button falls off it's time to buy a new shirt"

He rolled his eyes.

With Petunia's warm head rubbing against my leg, I watched the DI shuffle across the lawn and open the door of his car. My stomach gave a low-level gurgle. What if I did accidentally touch that gun? What if, while crawling around in amongst the soggy tea-bags, the half-eaten pies and the fly-blown chicken sandwiches, my hand brushed up against the murder weapon without me even knowing?

A cold lump squirmed in the center of my chest. I'd be arrested for murder. And there's no way my entire wedding party, plus the hundred guests Ma invited, would squeeze into a jail cell.

3

I DASHED THROUGH THE FRONT DOOR OF MY HOUSE, tossed two grubby dog rugs onto a nearby chair promising myself I'd wash them later, and let out a frustrated sigh. With only four days to my wedding, I had no time to worry about being arrested. No time to deal with the after-shocks of finding Mary Parker's dead body covered in slime-encrusted fish heads. Already I had an extensive to-do list which seemed to be growing daily. Like the final rehearsal of our wedding ceremony–I glanced at my watch – due to start on the sands of Semaphore beach in exactly seventeen and a half minutes.

Damn.

I closed my eyes and sucked in a deep breath that did absolutely nothing toward calming my pounding heart. If only I had time to let loose with a complete hissy-fit, scream and rant and find a softish-rock to kick, I know I'd feel better. But the ticking clock was against me. So, I swallowed two pain-killers with a glass of water, then galloped up the stairs to my bedroom to cover myself in perfume. Luckily, on my last visit to *The Luv Bug*, I bought a miniature spray-bottle, labelled *'Pheromones of the Soul'*. And just as well. Even after a long hot shower, decedent wafts of corpse-aroma still emanated from my traumatized pores and if pheromones couldn't override the pong–nothing could.

Before I could slip out the front door, my three house-dogs bailed me up, demanding attention. Tater, the cocky Chihuahua who thought he was a Doberman, Lucky the marshmallow-soft retired greyhound who loved playing with plush purple toys, and our recent addition to the household, Yolo, another retired greyhound. I'd been fostering Yolo when she almost died due to eating deliberately contaminated kibble. Naturally, I brought her inside the house to recover–and that's where she stayed.

After handing out a slice of cheese and a liver treat to each bouncing, smiling canine, I opened the back door, threw several colored balls out onto the fenced-in lawn and left them rocketing around, barking and doing burn-outs as if they hadn't seen the open air for three weeks instead of three hours.

Then, with seven minutes left to the start of my wedding rehearsal and at least a twenty-five- minute drive to Semaphore beach, I hit the road.

The reasons Ben and I decided to say our wedding vows on the beach instead of in a church, were twofold. One, we both loved the beach, and the bigee, we thought we could get away with dressing more casually. An idea my mother quickly vetoed. No daughter of hers was getting married in jeans, long boots and a fringed western top. Hence, even though it was a beach wedding, the bride was dressing in traditional white and the groom in a brand-new suit.

As I screeched to a halt in the Semaphore car park and then plowed through knee-deep seaweed on my way to the water's edge where the other members of my wedding party waited, I prayed our wacky marriage celebrant could keep her end of the bargain. Yeah, Delta Goodapple, a friend of my equally wacky sister, Liz, professed to be a fourth-generation witch. A witch who proclaimed with great solemnity that on Saturday morning, at 4.30am, when I would be walking down the aisle, the tides would be in perfect alignment, the mountains of seaweed would be washed back into the sea, the sun would be peeping over the horizon and all dark rain clouds would be banished to wherever rain clouds go when they're surplus to requirements.

I trudged on, constantly sinking into masses and masses of the slimy brown stuff. Four days for a wall of fishy-smelling seaweed to be washed away to sea? Our witchy celebrant would need a pretty damn good wand to honor that promise.

Puffing from the exertion, I stopped for a quick breath and waved to my family and friends who were milling around near the water's edge.

Ben and his older brother Nick–his best man–both dressed in scruffy jeans, work boots and checked flannel shirts, waved back. They must have come straight from rounding up and branding Nick's new calves on their Dad's farm. Dwarfed between them, Ma shouted at me to hurry up, I was late. As if I didn't know.

Jake, my dreadlocked, hippie kennel-assistant, dressed in his usual stand-out gear of bright red baggy trousers and purple jacket, was standing-in for my sister, Liz, who was one of my bridesmaids. She and her boyfriend, Scott, weren't due to arrive until the day before the wedding.

I could see Tanya, my Maid of Honor, attempting to foster a conversation with Delta the dreamy witch and failing to break through her spiritual meditation. Tanya was probably trying to con my marriage celebrant into buying something naughty at *The Luv Bug* to complement her magic powers.

And standing, or should I say staggering, a few feet from the rest, his mobile phone plastered to his ear, was my crazy Uncle Tony–known in the bottom echelon of lawyers as, Anthony Hamilton Jr. Ma's kid brother, a hopeless white-collar lawyer and an even more hopeless drunk, had been allotted the job of 'giving me away'.

For a moment I felt tears threaten as I thought of my father who wouldn't be here to 'give' me to Ben on Saturday. Alex McKinley had been run over and killed by a road-train almost six years ago. Until he died, Dad had been the cement that held our dysfunctional family together. Or so I'd thought, until six months ago when Attila the Hun, our domineering mother, confessed she wasn't our biological mother at all. Evidently Ma couldn't have children so paid her younger sister, our Aunty Sharon, to have a baby with Dad. The result was me…Katrina McKinley. However, my sister, Liz, was evidently the result of a clandestine love affair between Dad and Aunty Sharon, seven years later. They were going to run away together but Aunty Sharon died giving birth to Liz. And inexplicably, Ma took both Dad and the baby back home with her from the hospital.

My weird family…

But, hey, I loved them all.

"Sorry I'm late. Got held up," I told them, wheezing a little as I lurched out of the seaweed.

"So we heard." My gorgeous, soon-to-be-husband, Ben, moved toward me, both arms outstretched. I stepped straight in for a hug.

"What's this about you finding another dead body?" Ma, bristling with reproach, as if I'd found the body in the dumpster just to spite her, aimed a stink-eye frown in my direction. Her eyes flashed. "Katrina McKinley," she said, enunciating each syllable so I knew she meant business, "I do *not* want you getting involved in this woman's murder."

I shrugged one shoulder. "Hey, why would I want to? Mary Parker was a slut."

"But you knew her and that's usually enough reason," she persisted, latching on like a dog with a bone. "Remember, you have a wedding to prepare for, so there's no time for sleuthing."

I rolled my eyes at her. "Ma, stop stressing. I wouldn't cross the road to find this woman's killer."

"Come on, Kat, that's a bit harsh," said Ben, lifting an eyebrow at me. "Mary was okay, when you got to know her."

"Whaaat?" I pulled out of his arms and recoiled, hands on hips, ready to sting like a very angry wasp if this conversation went the wrong way. I shook my head at him. Just how well did Ben know Mary? How could he stick up for a woman who continually tried to break up our relationship?

"What I'm saying is she might have been a man-eater on the outside but underneath those slutty clothes, Mary was actually a rather nice person who'd had a very hard life."

"And of course, *you'd* know all about what she was like *under* her slutty clothes, wouldn't you?"

Ben lifted one eyebrow and there was a trace of hurt in his eyes. "Before you and I became an item, yes, I went out with Mary a few times."

I'd forgotten about Ben's many conquests before he settled down with me. Or maybe I'd just pushed that period of his life to the back of my mind, afraid I might never be enough woman for him. Benjamin Taylor had once been greyhound racing's sizzling hot bachelor. A serial dater who sometimes took two women out at the same time. I gritted my teeth in a snarl and growled low in my throat at the thought of Mary Parker's paws on any part of my man's body.

"We only lasted a couple of dates," he went on as if I hadn't turned into a green-eyed monster ready to pluck his eyes out if he said the wrong thing. "She was too much like hard work." He took my hand in his and squeezed. "Did you know Mary was once a victim of domestic violence? That her brute of a partner put her in hospital eight times and the last time, while she was in there recovering from a broken jaw, he got legless drunk and drove his car over a cliff with their three-year-old daughter fastened into the back seat?"

A lump clogged my throat making it hard to swallow. Mary had a baby daughter? How come I didn't know anything about this? *Because you're so jealous of Ben you don't look further than your nose*, a little voice in my head replied with an eye-roll.

Relentlessly, Ben continued on. "The car burst into flames and they were both incinerated. The little girl, Sally, I think she called her, was the light of Mary's life and she never got over losing her. I guess that's *why* she became a woman who didn't care what anyone thought of her. *And* why she basically hated men and used her body and her wiles to pump them up and then hurt them with rejection and contempt."

"And I was always so horrible to her." I closed my eyes. "Why didn't you tell me this before? Now I feel awful."

"It's not always just about you, Kat." Ben's voice was gentle.

"Oh God, I'm so sorry." What did Ben see in me? I was a bad person who thought of no one but herself. Maybe I should care about Mary being snuffed out by another coldhearted brute and investigate her murder after all. Maybe I should show her more compassion in death than I ever did in life.

Ben dragged me up against the soft flannel of his shirt which smelled of pee and frightened calf. "You didn't know about Mary's past life, Kat. How could you?" He frowned, the little crinkles in his forehead begging me to kiss each and every one of them. "But that doesn't mean it's *your* job to find her killer. We're getting hitched on Saturday so–no sleuthing. Right?"

I sent him a teary smile. The man could read minds.

"Come here, babe." His lips, soft and warm met mine. I closed my eyes and breathed in the tangy smell of farmyard, luxuriating in the knowledge that this man was mine. All mine. And I loved him. Moaning, I opened my mouth and prepared to partake in a little sexual exploration, involving tongues.

After what felt like ten minutes but was probably only two, Tanya poked me in the ribs, which I ignored. "Jesus guys! Get a room!"

"Yeah," put in Nick covering his eyes in mock embarrassment. "Can you please leave off eating each other? At least until we get this rehearsal over and dusted?"

Tanya gave me another poke. This time, harder, deeper and more insistent. "Hey, I'm on a tight schedule here. I'm due to start my shift at *The Luv Bug* in less than an hour, plus, in case you've forgotten, your marriage celebrant, the magical Delta Goodapple gets paid by the minute and because you were late, we're already half an hour into her session."

My lips, swollen and sated, reluctantly unplugged at the mention of where we were, what we were supposed to be there for and how much it was costing us.

"Later," Ben promised as, eyes never leaving mine, he slowly licked my taste from his lips.

Reluctantly pushing through my sexual fog I looked around and blinked. "But we can't start without Jules? And where's Erin, my flower girl?"

"Sorry, Erin's gone on a school trip to Monarto Zoo. I'm afraid lions and giraffes outscored, in her words, 'a boring old wedding rehearsal'," said Tanya whose eleven-year-old daughter was to be my flower girl.

"Jules not with you?" Ma frowned at me. "She's never late. When she didn't turn up on time, I thought maybe she was hitching a ride with you."

I shook my head, equally worried. "The last thing Jules said to me when I left the track today was she'd see me at the wedding rehearsal at four."

"Well we can't wait any longer," growled Uncle Toby. "My time is valuable. I should be with…um…you know, an important client." I turned around to find my uncle staggering as he shoved his phone back into his pocket and exchanged it with what looked like a hip flask. Even from a few feet away, I could smell alcohol on his breath.

Ma, his older sister, glared at him. "Oh, for Pete's sake, Anthony, put that booze away and stop whining." She fisted her hands on her hips and leant forward in her favorite Attila the Hun pose. "I'm telling you now, if you arrive at my daughter's wedding on Saturday morning smelling like a brewery, I'll emasculate you on the spot with a blunt kitchen knife."

All talking ceased.

Uncle Tony blinked at my mother and, knowing she was quite capable of carrying out her threat, stuffed the hip flask back into his pocket and backed away until he was ankle deep in the sea.

It was Tanya who finally broke the awed silence. She gave a fake cough and jabbed a finger into the wedding celebrant, who seemed to be either meditating or silently conversing with each and every one of the white fluffy clouds sprinkled across the blue sky. "Maybe Jules has car trouble," she said. "We'll have to start without her."

Delta blinked several times as though she'd been in another world–a world more peaceful and magical than this one–and was grudgingly returning to the beach and our dysfunctional wedding rehearsal. "Um…right, ladies and gentlemen, are you ready now?" Not waiting for a reply, Delta took in a deep breath, and then continued. "Please move quietly into your allotted positions, like I showed you last time, and we'll get the bride and groom mock-married for the third time this month."

There was a shuffling of feet as everyone moved into place. Ben and Nick on Delta's left, Mum on her right and after helping Uncle Tony out of the sea and wringing out the cuffs of his trousers, Tanya, Jake and I moved further down the beach in preparation for the wedding march.

"Okay," Delta said and started humming. "Dum. Dum. Da dum. Dum. Dum. Da dum."

I watched Tanya and Jake, who was standing in for Liz as bridesmaid number one, parade down the beach in front of me and grinned at the mischievous way Jake wriggled his rear end with every stride.

"Come on, Kat." Delta broke into my snorting amusement. "That's your cue to move too."

Woops. I took one step forward and brought my feet together and another step and brought my feet together, as I'd been instructed, and suddenly realized I had no 'father of the bride' moving down the aisle beside me. I looked around and came to a halt.

Uncle Tony stood with his back to me, mobile phone plastered to his ear. "A hundred big ones on number four in the last race at Morphetville. Yeah, yeah, Andre, I'll fix you up next week. No worries, man." He looked around, saw me watching him and covering the receiver with one hand, waved me on with the other. "Um…sorry, kid. I'll catch you up. Important call."

By now we had an audience. A man and his rather vocal dog which was running loose, barking and goosing people, three giggly teenage girls whose eyes were feasting on the dreadlocked Jake, and a bikini clad woman with an ADD toddler who kept filling his little red plastic bucket with sea water and throwing it at us.

Maybe Ma had a point when she said there'd be a lot more privacy if we married in a church.

"Anthony!" Mum's roar disturbed a squadron of seagulls who'd also gathered to watch proceedings. "You moron. I'm coming after you and I have a large pair of scissors in my bag!" The birds flew off squawking, Uncle Tony dropped his mobile and ran into the sea, the dog followed him all the while trying to goose him in the rear, and the bucket-toting toddler giggled so much he finally succumbed to hiccups.

I rolled my eyes at Tanya who was bent double pretending to retie a shoe that had no laces, while in reality she was almost wetting her pants. I sighed. "They say a bad rehearsal means a successful opening night. Right?"

Tanya straightened up, wiping tears from her eyes. She tried to talk but evidently too choked up, couldn't get any words out.

I looked at Jake. "Right?" I repeated, this time, louder.

Jake, the twenty or so silver rings and studs embedded in his nose, ear-lobes, lips, and chin jiggling with each belly-laugh, looked up, white teeth flashing. "Yeah, man. That's right."

There was a sudden deep animal-like growl that stopped us all in our stride. I looked across to see our witchy wedding celebrant, her face the color of ripe plums, one hand draped across her temples in an I-can't-possibly-cope-with-this-any-longer, dramatic pose. "We're here to rehearse for a wedding–not a bad Noel Coward play," she growled, her eyes turning into snake-slits. The growl in her throat grew louder and louder until I thought she was going to explode into a hundred zillion pieces right there on the yellow strip of sand between the seaweed and the waves.

I threw myself at Ben, who dragged me closer. Horrified, yet unable to look away, we stared at Delta Goodapple as she raised her scrawny arms to the heavens, her eyes spinning in their sockets.

"Crap," said Ben, his voice cracking. "I think the crazy witch is going to turn us all into toads."

"Not me!" yelled Tanya. She snaffled her tote bag from where she'd left it perched on a nearby pile of seaweed and took off up the beach. "I'm out of here!"

Delta's growling turned into a guttural chant deep in her throat. Her eyes spun like a fun-fair ride. "Urglefurkle. Gunngadurkle. Sham. Sham. Gaaaaaaah…"

Instantly the sky darkened to night. Gale force winds sprung out of nowhere, lifting the sand and spiraling it into the air. And hailstones as big and solid as marbles rained down from the skies.

The bikini-clad mother grabbed her toddler under one arm and sprinted for the car park. The guy whistled the dog and took off up the beach, hands protecting his head. While my wedding party scattered and ran screaming toward their vehicles.

"Holy catfish!" I gasped as Ben and I raced hand in hand toward the shelter of our cars, yelping each time the icy hailstones bit into our exposed skin. "No way will I ever piss that woman off again!"

The moment we hit the bitumen of the carpark, Ben lifted me off the ground and threw me into the safety of his van.

"Better still, babe," he shouted in my ear, "let's just elope!"

4

THOR THE GOD OF THUNDER ROARED FROM THE TOP OF Mt Olympus as thousands of jagged lightning strikes broke the sky apart.

Cuddled up against Ben, I watched the hailstones pummel the windscreen, heard them bounce off the roof like gunshots as I snuggled closer into the warmth of his flannel shirt.

"You okay, babe?"

I nodded, eyes on the frozen marbles that hit the windscreen and slid down onto the bonnet of the van, leaving a fast-growing drift of melting white. "Yeah, but I wouldn't like to be outside the car now. Look at the size of those monsters. They'd leave you more bruised than a boxer after a Championship fight." I waited while Thor let out another angry roar of displeasure overhead. "Do you really think our wacky marriage celebrant created this?"

"Wouldn't put it past her," he said. "But that's not what I meant. Are you okay after finding Mary's body? Why didn't you ring me? I'd have left Nick to his scrawny piddling calves and rushed to the track to be with you. You know that."

I hadn't thought to ring Ben at the time. Why? Was that a sign I didn't need him? That he wasn't important enough in my life to ask for his help when I was in trouble? Was I really ready to get married? "Guess I was just too numb to think straight at the time," I mumbled. "And after that, I pushed the thought of Mary to the back of my mind. What with our wedding rehearsal, the final fitting of my wedding dress in an hour's time and dealing with Ma and the last-minute catering arrangements, I haven't had time to get my head around it all yet."

"As I said, I'm happy to elope. Or we could just drive to the nearest registry office right now, sign whatever forms are needed to get hitched, and then take off for our honeymoon a couple of days early."

"In these dripping wet clothes?" I laughed as I shook my head and rain showered from my hair like confetti. "And can you imagine the excruciating pain my mother would inflict on your two most cherished possessions if you told her the wedding ceremony was off because we were already married? She's barely accepted the fact we're getting married on the beach instead of a church–but a registry office, without the fanfare and traditional ceremony? Your boys would be toast, Benjamin."

Ben wriggled in his seat. "Hey, they're shrinking in fear at the thought." And then his fingers closed over mine and he dropped a soft kiss on the top of my head. "To be honest, I don't care how or where we get married. I just know I want to spend the rest of my life with you."

Awww! And that's when I realized how stupid I'd been. How I'd let wedding nerves scramble the gray matter in my cranium. Of course I wanted to marry Ben–he was the yin to my yang. Heck, I'd gagged for the guy from the very first moment I'd laid eyes on him at the dog track. There he was striding around on the lawn like a movie star, toileting six dogs before kenneling and chatting away to them as though they were human. He even produced a packet of small black degradable plastic bags from his pocket which he used to pick up the dog poo before depositing it in the bin provided. How sweet was that? And I remember right from the start how Benjamin Taylor, at that time, greyhound racing's most eligible bad boy bachelor, had knocked me right out of the ballpark with his smile. The guy was so leg-meltingly handsome, so freaking hot, I'd gone home and dreamed of ripping off his clothes and having my way with him on every conceivable surface.

Yet, for the first six months of our relationship, Ben treated me just like one of the guys. Which meant while I contemplated dancing naked on the bonnet of my car–just so he'd see me as a woman with boobs and all the other necessary equipment–he was happy to be a good mate. Someone to knock around with, chew the fat, play a few games of pool, borrow a jar of heat-rub when he'd run out.

After returning his kiss with something a bit more solid than a soft touch on the top of the head, I told Ben about DI Adam's visit and how the police had found the murder weapon in the dumpster next to Mary's body. "What if it wasn't murder?" I said, glass-half-full. "What if Mary climbed in the dumpster and then shot herself? Committed suicide because everyone hated her?"

"Nah. Not Mary's style. No matter what life threw at her she'd kick butt and tough it out. No way would she end her own life because a few trolls heckled her on Facebook."

I screwed up my nose. "S'pose you're right. Plus I can't see Mary snuffing herself in a smelly garbage bin. If Mary decided to commit suicide she'd turn it into a front-page drama. You know, ring the Channel Seven News team and invite them all down with their cameras to televise the event."

"And she'd take a full-page ad in the newspaper to let everyone know the exact date and time." Ben heaved a sigh and pulled me closer. He knew I was making light of Mary's death as a way of coping. He knew I was having trouble coming to terms with finding someone I knew personally, stiff and cold, their essence, their life-form, gone forever, dead inside a dumpster.

Arms wrapped around me, he drew me closer, enfolding me in a Ben-like hug. I lay the side of my face against his heart and listened to the strong regular beat, accepting the strength he offered me. One thing my Ben excelled at was giving hugs where you can actually feel the sadness leave your body.

"So," I said when the hug finished and I leant back against the car seat and listened to the hailstones ping against the car roof. "Who do *you* think murdered Mary?"

"The way she's been pissing everyone off over the last year or two, the question isn't *who* would kill her–but who *wouldn't*. Mary's been the cause of so many relationship break-ups I'm surprised her exploits haven't been listed in the Guinness Book of Records." He shrugged. "It was all just a game to her."

"But would jealousy be enough motive for murder? Okay, every time she made a pass at you, right under my nose, I'd get spitting mad and want to yank her hair out–but I'd never react by picking up a gun and shooting her. What would be the point of that? One, I don't look good in prison stripes and two, what sort of relationship could we build together if I was behind bars for the next twenty-odd years?"

"Mary's murderer is extremely dangerous, Kat. So don't get involved. Whoever killed Mary, for whatever reason, will kill again rather than get caught and locked up."

"Don't worry, Sweetcheeks. In case you've forgotten, I have a wedding to attend at sunrise on Saturday morning."

"*Sweetcheeks?*"

I cut him a wicked grin, just to let him know exactly which cheeks I considered sweet. "And for the three days leading up to that wedding, I'll be too busy to blow my nose let alone become involved in any sleuthing." I lifted my eyebrows at him in what I considered a come-hither look. "Plus, after Saturday, I'll be too busy servicing my new husband."

"Roll on Saturday." With his fingers playing in my hair, he let out a deep heartfelt sigh. "Jesus, Kat, how am I supposed to get through the next few nights without you?"

"No fun for me either."

"Are you absolutely sure your grandmother has to stay with you?"

"Yep. It's Ma's way of keeping you and me apart until our wedding night." I stifled a laugh at the thought of all those nights Ben and I had rolled around on my bed together, the Kama Sutra beside us on the bedside table. We'd follow intricate diagrams, laugh, forget the next step and just go for it anyway. Totally and unselfconsciously in love. But with Grandma Hamilton, Ma's mother, the Dragon of all Dragons, keeping watch over me until our wedding day, Ben's presence at my house would be on a work-only basis. Grandma Hamilton was the woman who accompanied her two daughters, Ma and Aunty Sharon, on every date until they were almost of marriageable age.

"When does the dragon arrive?"

"Tonight. Ma's also arranged for her to house-sit until we get back from our honeymoon."

Ben put on his best puppy-dog face, all big eyes and panting tongue. "Win that case, what say we race home and have a quickie before she arrives?"

I leant forward and deposited a brief peck on his cheek. "Sorry, Benjamin, but the rain has stopped. The sky is blue again. And I have my last fitting with the dressmaker on the outskirts of Two Wells in exactly fifty-three minutes."

And with that, I opened the door of the van, stepped out into an ankle-deep puddle and splashed my way across the car park toward my station-wagon.

5

An hour and a half later, I stood in the middle of my dressmaker's lounge room, both arms lifted out to the side, while she stretched the tape measure around my bust. This was my last pre-wedding appointment of the day. The final fitting of my wedding gown–the very same gown my mother wore when she married my dad all those years ago. I'd always loved the dress. It was beautiful. And I remember, as a kid, touching the silky material with reverence the few times Ma took it out of its protective wrapping.

As usual, my mother had beaten me to the dressmaker's house and was now running around like an over-medicated teenager supervising the fitting. That's if you can call hating every change Gloria made to the dress, raiding the poor woman's biscuit tin, pouring cups of coffee without asking permission and generally stirring me up, as supervising.

Bridal fittings in books and movies are usually depicted as happy girlie things where the bride and her bridesmaids gossip, laugh and tease each other, all while sipping champagne. Not this bridal fitting. It was just Ma and me. Tanya and Erin's dresses were already completed, wrapped in plastic, and hanging in their wardrobes–a gorgeous lemony-lime for Erin and a slinky cerulean blue for Tanya. As my sister, Liz, was unavailable for a fitting, Gloria made her dress by using me for a model. On the assumption that Liz and I were of a similar size.

Once again, Jules, whose dress wasn't quite finished, was a no-show. I was starting to worry about her. She wasn't answering her mobile and even though I'd left several messages for her to return my call, there'd been no reply. Maybe she'd been called out on a personal emergency, and in her hurry, left her mobile behind. But it wasn't like Jules to be forgetful.

I was in the middle of telling the dressmaker about how our rehearsal on Semaphore beach came to an abrupt end, when Ma interrupted. "Don't be ridiculous, Katrina," she said, shaking her head so hard I expected the clips holding her bun in place to go flying in the air and land in the middle of her coffee. "You're making it sound like your weird wedding celebrant instigated the storm."

"But didn't you see–"

"It was merely a coincidence. A freak storm that came out of nowhere. That strange woman your dizzy sister recommended does *not* have special powers."

"Well, how do you explain the way–"

"Surely you don't believe Delta Goodapple is a witch?" she broke in again, adding a loud tut. "Witches only inhabit fairy tales."

"But Ma–"

"However, if you and Ben were to change your minds and get married in a church, by a good Christian minister…"

Here we go again. I let out a sigh and tuned Ma's voice out. Instead, dressed in white silk and heritage lace, I succumbed to the pulling and poking and pinning as my dressmaker worked on the final tiny adjustments to my wedding dress. Ma might call it a coincidence, but I still couldn't get my head around the storm at Semaphore beach which lasted precisely eight minutes, and when it abated, miraculously left the sky as blue as a baby boy's romper suit. One eye on the clock, I shuffled from one foot to the other, silently urging the woman to hurry up as it was now almost 5.30pm which meant all my dogs would be enquiring, rather noisily, re exactly what time they were going to be fed.

The dressmaker, Miss Gloria Tremaine, was a pinched prune of a woman in her mid-forties. However, her perpetually tightened lips, long nose that seemed to always be smelling something nasty and her hard little button eyes made her appear much older. The biggest gossip in the whole of Two Wells and Gawler combined, Gloria cocked one ear as she made a slight alteration to the bodice of my gown and was so intent on nodding in agreement while my mother ranted on about Ben and me not getting married in a church, she stuck me in the left breast with a pin.

"Ouch! Watch it!"

"Sorry."

"Ben won't be happy if you damage the merchandise." I grinned at her and winked. Hey, we were all women here and anyway, I needed practice for my upcoming Hen's party. "You see, he's rather partial to feasting on my boobs before moving lower."

Gloria's cheeks turned bright red and her eyes widened in horror at the mention of boobs and other bedroom shenanigans. Sheesh! Unmarried herself, I wondered if Gloria's only sexual adventures came from reading sweet Mills and Boon romances.

"Um…so…y-you're not getting married in a church?" she squeaked, abruptly changing the subject.

"No, the ceremony is being performed on a public beach, chock full of seaweed and dicey tides," Ma answered for me, completely ignoring my bedroom talk. Guess foreplay was all old hat to her and anyway she probably didn't want to contaminate my mind with thoughts of parental sex. "However," she continued, eyeing me like an insect she'd like to spray, "this *is* Katrina's wedding. *She* makes the decisions. So, I'm not saying any more. I'm not one of those annoying mothers who interfere in their daughter's life."

I almost swallowed my tongue at that one. In fact, I had to chow down hard on my bottom lip to stop from laughing out loud. No wonder so many couples skip the wedding ceremony and just shift in together. If I'd known how much stress weddings involved, I'd have taken up Ben's offer to, 'just elope'.

Gloria, now kneeling on the floor to put the final touches to the hem of my white lacy wedding gown, looked up at me. "I heard you found Mary Parker's body."

I closed my eyes and my stomach sank. Please don't go there.

"What did she look like?"

I frowned. What did she think she looked like? "Very dead." I ran a hand down my arm, smoothing the lace on my left sleeve. I didn't want to think about Mary's lifeless face with her empty staring eyes. And I certainly didn't want to talk about it.

Gloria's lips twisted and I thought for one insane moment she was going to spit on the floor. "Got her comeuppance, I say."

I stared down at the dressmaker whose thin pinched lips were puckered into a moue of distaste. "Mary was murdered, Gloria. Murdered. No-one deserves to be murdered." It was okay for me to call Mary names, but not an outsider. Someone not part of the greyhound industry. Plus, after finding out about Mary's past life I was becoming a little protective of her.

Gloria sniffed. "Did you know a friend of mine contemplated suicide because of that tramp?" She didn't wait for an answer but continued on, her voice laced with venom. "Mary Parker stole my friend's fiancé and then, when confronted, laughed in her face."

"She evidently did that a lot." My mother decided to join in the juicy conversation even though she'd never set eyes on the deceased.

"And then she lured him into her bed." Gloria's eyes hardened. "My friend found out and broke up with him. And do you know what Mary Parker did then? She ditched him and moved on to someone else's man."

I frowned down at the dressmaker who was sticking pins into the hem of my dress with abandon–as though sticking pins in Mary Parker's eyes. "Hopefully your friend didn't forgive her fiancé and take him back?"

"She tried, but he spurned her." Gloria's shoulders sagged and she pushed herself up off the floor. "By then, he'd been warped, twisted by that Jessabelle's poison."

I frowned. The little dressmaker was making me feel a tad uncomfortable with her deep well of animosity. *For a friend's problem?* "Um. Sorry to hear that. Hope your friend got over him quickly and moved on."

"He told my friend that after having *real* sex with Mary, there was no way he could go back to a cold wet fish with ice for a libido. And then he walked away."

I raised my eyebrows at Ma who pulled an 'Oh sheet!' face behind Gloria's back in return. Sounded like the 'friend' could be Gloria herself? If so, no wonder the little dressmaker had the look of a shirt left in the starch water too long. I softened my voice as she turned her back and made a big deal out of stabbing the left-over pins into a pin-cushion. "If you don't mind me saying so, Gloria, your friend is better off without him. Any man who would say that to a woman, isn't worth another thought. Your friend should have hung the creep by his balls, upside down in a tree infested with bull ants."

Gloria gave a thin-lipped smile–or maybe she had indigestion – and even Ma blinked at that one.

Before changing from my wedding finery back into damp street clothes, I grabbed my mobile from where I'd left it on top of the antique dresser at the back of the room. Most of Gloria's furniture suited the setting of the hundred-year-old cottage perfectly. Furniture she must have collected from auctions and antique shops and then lovingly restored.

By now my dogs were probably lifting the roof off the kennel house with their demands to be fed, but I had to try to reach Jules one more time. This was so unlike her. My friend, Jules, was whatever you call the opposite to a flibbertigibbet. Even my mother approved of her. Responsible. Always on time. Never klutzy. And she could shoot the eye out of a potato at a hundred paces.

Before I could click on her number, the phone rang. I lifted the cell to my ear and frowned. It was Jules, but the voice on the other end sounded so unlike her, so shrill, so confused, I had to make sure. "Jules?"

"Kat, I'm in deep shit."

"Calm down. Where are you? I've been trying to get in touch with you for the last two hours. You forgot the wedding rehearsal and your final fitting. Not that you missed much–the rehearsal was a complete stuff-up, but–"

"They took my mobile away."

"Who took your mobile? Where are you? Jules, you're not making a lot of sense."

"I'm at the Elizabeth police station." Her voice quavered slightly, which once again, was not like my friend who was so tough I often accused her of eating live spiders for breakfast. "Kat…what am I going to do? I've been charged with the murder of Mary Parker."

I tried to grab a breath but there didn't seem to be enough air in the room. It was like someone had punched me in the gut and then finished me off with a roundhouse kick to the head. "But-but why? Why would the police do that?"

"Because Mary Parker was shot with one of my guns."

6

Not only was Jules a good friend–she was also my bridesmaid. I'd need her to walk down the aisle in front of me in four days' time. So, the fact that she'd been charged with murder and incarcerated in a jail cell turned my resolve to keep out of the case completely on its ear.

Back home again, I did the evening chow-run which involved feeding the racing dogs, GAP dogs and house-dogs, gave each of the racers a run in the paddock and then joined Ben in the treatment room—a small well-equipped room adjacent to the newly extended kennel house. Ben was giving Lofty and Clark a short tepid hydro-bath to relax their muscles after racing.

My brain still puzzling over who could have framed Jules for murder–by using her gun to kill Mary–I perched on a three-legged stool beside the hydro-bath. Clark, a bouncy fawn greyhound known at the racetrack as Wonder Boy, stood beside me. Already bathed and dried, Clark leaned against my leg and while I scratched him behind his ears he tipped his head on one side and gave me a dreamy-eyed smile. If he'd been a cat he'd be purring.

"Ten bucks for them, babe." Ben, stooped over big goofy Lofty while toweling him dry, broke into my musings.

"Ten bucks for what?"

"Your thoughts," he said and lifted one eyebrow. "You were miles away I've asked you three times to pass me the blow dryer so I can finish this boy off."

I stood up, disturbing a disgruntled Clark and passed Ben the hair-dryer. Since Jules' phone conversation at the dressmakers, I'd been deep inside my head, merely going through the motions of everyday life. Jules charged with murder? It didn't make sense. She wasn't even in a relationship at the moment, so what motive would she have to kill Mary?

With an effort I forced myself back into the present. "Just shows how much the cost of living has gone up from our grandmother's day. Grandma McKinley only ever offers me a penny for them, yet you're ready to part with ten bucks."

"Figuratively, my love." He tied Lofty to the brass ring in the wall, plugged in the hair dryer and switched it on. "By the look on your face your thoughts are all about Jules."

"Who else?" I raised my voice over the whirring of the hair dryer. "The police found Jules' gun in the dumpster. Now I ask you, why would she shoot Mary then toss her gun, which would incriminate her, into the dumpster for the police to find?" I shook my head. To me the police were acting dumber than a crate of empty beer bottles. "No self-respecting killer would leave their gun next to the body, would they? Add to that," I continued, so frustrated I almost kicked the wall but the wall was made of brick and my foot wasn't. "Uncle Tony, her temporary-counsel, went through all the normal channels, but he couldn't get her out on bail."

"Sorry, Kat, but your Uncle Tony couldn't get the Queen out on bail."

"I know, but he's only filling in for John Patterson, the firm's top criminal lawyer," I told him. "Hopefully, when John gets back from the Bahamas on Friday, he'll boot Uncle Tony to the curb and get Jules out of jail in time for our wedding on Saturday."

"We can only hope."

"If not, I have a feeling Ma will do the booting to the curb and take over from Uncle Tony herself. She's having kittens worrying about me coming down the aisle with no bridesmaids." I shrugged one shoulder. "We haven't heard from my sister, Liz, since last week, so who knows whether *she'll* arrive in time for the wedding."

Ben finished drying Lofty, turned the hairdryer off and gazed across at me, love in the smile that crinkled his eyes. "As long as you're there, babe, I don't care if no one else shows up."

"Aw. That's *so* sweet." What a gorgeous guy. I could eat him all up.

His crinkly grin turned wicked and his eyes predatory. "Sweet? Sweet? I'm *so* not sweet.' One arm shot out and hooked me behind the knees making me lose my balance and topple back against him. "Come here, woman, and I'll show you how *un*sweet I am."

Laughing, Ben lifted me up on the stool and before I could get away, had me in an arm-lock. "Still think I'm sweet?"

"Sweeter than a bowl full of pink and yellow M&M's topped with cherry flavored ice-cream."

"Hoohoo! You're for it now. I'm going to tickle you mercilessly until you yell, 'Ben Taylor is one tough dangerous dude'.

"Never!"

A tussle ensued, whereby arms, legs and tickling fingers jumbled with hot lips, wandering hands and plunging tongues. Lofty, tied to the ring on the wall, barked as if to say, 'Come on, guys, let me join in too!' while Clark, now loose in the room, spun around in circles, barking and showing off like a toddler on a caffeine-high.

Ben had me rolling on the ground, giggling hysterically, shirt up around my neck, tickling and kissing my bare skin when the door of the treatment room burst open.

And Ma and her dragon of a mother stood framed in the doorway.

I let out a yelp. "Ma? Gran?"

Neither woman spoke.

"Um… Sorry, forgot you were coming." No, that didn't sound right. Face hot, I quickly pushed my shirt down, shoved Ben off of me and staggered to my feet. "Gran, it's so lovely to see you again. Why, it must be a month since we visited you at *Resthaven*."

"Actually, it's three."

"Um…right." I grabbed the end of Clark's lead and twisted it around my fingers before he discovered the door was open and decided to go walkabout. How could I have forgotten Ma was picking Gran up from the train station at seven o'clock? And more importantly, that she was bringing her straight here?

Now in her eighties, Gran had always been straight-laced, a veritable virago, who held morals entrenched in the dim dark ages. One of them being–if a woman wasn't a virgin on her wedding night, she must be a prostitute. And her beady eyes were currently zeroing in on my shirt. I glanced down to find four of my six buttons undone. Aaagh. I grit my teeth. I was so not going to embarrass myself further by doing them up while she watched. Hey, it was time Gran dragged her mind kicking and screaming into *this* century.

Instead, with a flick of my hand, I indicated Ben who was still rearranging his clothing. "Gran, this is my fiancé, Benjamin Taylor. Ben, this is Ma's mother, Granny Hamilton."

Ben dithered for a moment with a should-I-give-her-a-peck-on-the-cheek-or-should-I-shake-hands expression on his face. Finally. he wiped one hand on the seat of his jeans and held it out. "G'day Mrs. Hamilton. Kat's told me all about you."

"I'm sure she has." Gran frowned at his outstretched hand, gingerly touched it with the tip of one finger and quickly brought her arm back to her side.

As she did so, a raspy cough came from behind her and from out of nowhere, a hunched up old man on a walking frame, twinkling eyes at least five decades younger than the rest of his body, shuffled around Granny Hamilton and clunked into the room.

I blinked at him. An apparition? A passing motorist whose car broke down and he needed a phone? "Can I help you?"

"Well, well, what have we here?" The scarecrow clumped all the way into the room and regarded our disheveled appearance with a lift of one eyebrow. "These must be the two love birds getting hitched on Saturday?" Not waiting for an answer, he continued, faded blue eyes brimming with amusement. "I'm Fred. Fred Boner. I live in the same retirement village as your Gran." His toothy grin fell on me. "Katrina, isn't it?"

I nodded.

"Well, Katrina, my dear, I hope you don't mind putting me up in your sweet little house, along with your Gran for a week." His grin widened, causing the leathery wrinkles that made up a large percentage of his face, to deepen. "We come as a pair, so there's no need to trouble yourself by preparing two rooms. I'll sleep with Veronica." He turned to Gran whose cheeks shone with two bright splotches of red. "After all, she's my honey." He threw one arm around Gran and tugged her closer. "Isn't that right, Snugglepie?"

Snugglepie? I blinked. No way could my prune-faced Gran be anyone's *Snugglepie*. It was biologically and emotionally impossible. I could feel Ben behind me. His whole body shaking as though trying desperately not to laugh out loud. "So…Fred," I said. "You want to stay here with Gran?"

I *really* needed to make sure of the facts before reacting.

"Bingo. And don't worry, my dear, I'll keep little Vee locked up in our room and out of your hair." He raised one bushy eyebrow in Gran's direction. "She's one hot mamma, your grandma."

I tried to speak, found my mouth was already open, closed it again and forgot what I was going to say.

"I hope you don't mind, Katrina," Granny Hamilton rushed into the awkward silence that followed. She glanced across at Ma who had seemingly lost the power of speech, then smiled doe-eyed at the wrinkly old man with the bad-boy eyes. "Fred is so good with animals whereas I'm not accustomed to them, so he's going to help me house-sit while you and Ben are away on your honeymoon."

"Um…fine. That's fine," I croaked, refusing to let my imagination go anywhere near the picture of my wrinkled Gran as a hot mamma. "Yep. Definitely fine."

"And don't pay attention to Freddy." Gran smiled at the elfin-faced guy beside her and suddenly looked ten years younger and sort of beautiful–in an old lady sort of way. "He's always mislaying his filter." She shook her head at him with a mock-frown before continuing. "Whatever finds its way into Freddy's head doesn't hang around to gather moss–it tumbles straight out of his mouth again. A lot like vomit. But don't worry, he'll be no trouble. I'll keep him in line."

"Oooh, yeah," growled Fred, doing a little shuffle-ball-change dance while holding firmly to his walking frame for balance. "Don't you love it when she gets bossy?"

Gran leaned over and whispered something into Fred's ear. He let out a deep throated chuckle, just managing to catch his false teeth before they hit the ground. "Oh, you naughty girl!' he said and gave her a light smack on the derriere.

Gran giggled like a schoolgirl.

I closed my mouth with a decisive snap. No way did I want to know what *that* was all about. Then, on the grounds that my eyes might explode if I was subjected to any more of this X rated senior movie, I untied Lofty and decided to take both dogs back to their kennels.

With Ben struggling to keep a straight face beside me, I hurried toward the open doorway, where Ma stood, shoulders tense, a tight frown etched into the skin between her eyes. Poor Ma. She looked completely shell-shocked. And why wouldn't she be? Her straight-laced mother, taking no notice of her goggle-eyed audience, was now giggling and simpering like a star-struck teenager as Fred planted a series of love bites on her bare, corrugated-iron neck.

"I don't believe this," I heard Ma mutter as I ducked past her and made my way outside. "We don't visit your grandmother for three months and she not only *reads* 'Fifty Shades of Grey', she meets up with a wrinkly bad boy who thinks he's Christian Grey's grandfather."

After settling the dogs down for the night and making sure Ben was thoroughly kissed before seeing him off the premises, I kicked the gravel in front of me as I wandered back to the house. Not sure what I'd find. There was a light on in the kitchen. I could hear the house-dogs romping around in the back yard. And a delicious aroma of cooking drifted through the open front door. Smelled like spaghetti Bolognese.

"Just in time for dinner," said Gran as I walked into the kitchen, eyes half-closed in case the elderly lovers were eating dinner off each other.

Everything looked pretty normal, all clothes intact, so I washed my hands at the sink, dried them on a hand towel and looked around. Gran was busy grating cheese over three huge servings of spaghetti Bolognese while Fred had abandoned his walking frame and sat grinning at the kitchen table, knife in one hand, fork in the other.

Where did my grandmother find the ingredients for spaghetti Bolognese? Certainly not in *my* cupboards.

"Your Gran could have been a Gourmet Chef," Fred said almost drooling as a loaded plate arrived on the table in front of him. "She cooks like an angel."

"I don't get much chance to cook at our rule-obsessed retirement home. Every time I step foot in their kitchen they report me for some health and safety violation." Gran placed a steaming plate of food in front of me. "Here you go, Katrina. By the look of those bones sticking out of your shoulders you need fattening up. Cooking will be my pleasure over the next few days. And as you can see, I brought provisions with me. By the bareness of your cupboards and refrigerator, it's just as well I did."

I grinned up at her. Maybe this visit wasn't going to be the nightmare I expected. Before I left for my honeymoon, there'd be good home cooked meals, plus unexpected entertainment.

Gran dropped a sheet of paper containing a long list of groceries on the table beside my plate. "Now, Katrina, because of the emptiness of your cupboards and refrigerator I've listed a few things I'll need you to buy from the store for me." She wiped her hands on a hand towel, pulled out a chair and sat down behind the third well-heaped plate. "When I went hunting for some basil to add to my sauce, I found the larder only contained tins of dog food and the only part of your refrigerator stacked with food was your freezer." She shook her head at me. "Have you ever read the information on the back of one of those frozen meal boxes, Katrina? 900 mg of salt per serving. Do you know what that amount of salt eventually does to your kidneys?"

Um…no. And I really didn't want to. "This is delicious, Gran," I said, in attempt to divert her from her lecture.

"Shrivels them up and by the time you're fifty you'll need a kidney transplant. That's what salt does."

Fred looked up. He licked the sauce from around his mouth with a very-agile tongue. "What's this I hear about you being an amateur detective, Kat? Veronica tells me you've been instrumental in putting quite a few criminals behind bars."

"And very nearly got herself killed in the process." Gran added before turning to Fred and making sickly goo-goo eyes at him. "Freddy here used to be a top detective in the force, didn't you, darling?"

Fred, struggling to transfer several long strings of spaghetti from the plate to his mouth, nodded.

"*And* he received one of those bravery awards to prove it. Of course that was a long time ago. Way before his speech-filter went AWOL."

Fred, errant spaghetti successfully relocated and swallowed, turned to me. "Veronica tells me you found another dead body today."

I sniffed. "You make it sound like I stumble over dead bodies like other people trip over their shoe laces."

"Don't be silly, Katrina." Gran reached for the pepper pot and proceeded to blacken her meal. "This time, Fred can help you find the perpetrator. It's always handy to have an experienced detective to bounce ideas off and to watch your back."

"Any time," said Fred looking up from his plate. "In fact, it would be my pleasure."

I inspected the man who was offering to be my back-up against a killer. Frail, wizened, hunched over and absolutely no use to me in a fight at all–yet Fred exuded an energy, a life-force that people many years his junior would covet. "Sounds good to me," I told him, and somehow I meant it.

"That reminds me, I have some news for you," said Gran leaning forward, eyes bright. "Your friend, Jules, insists *two* of her guns are missing. She just hadn't got around to reporting the theft to the police."

Two guns? So there was still one gun unaccounted for. Scary. "Who told you?"

"Tony, of course."

"Uncle Tony shouldn't be giving you information, Gran. By doing so, he's breaking his client's confidentiality."

"But I'm his mother, Katrina. And if he doesn't tell *me* what I want to know *I'll* break his fingers." Once again, the years had fallen away leaving Gran as keen as a pot of mustard. Evidently a new beau plus becoming involved in this sleuthing business was akin to the fountain of youth.

"So, your friend was framed." Fred buttered a slice of bread, cut it in two and using one half, proceeded to wipe up the remaining sauce on his plate. "Couple things you need to consider in this case, Kat. If you can find out who stole the guns–you'll have your murderer. Ask around. Might be a witness who saw someone hanging around Jules' house at the time the guns went missing. And if not, ask yourself this question– who had a motive for killing the deceased?"

"The short answer to your second question is, 'a truckload of people. In fact, every woman who lost their partner to Mary had a motive."

"And was your friend Jules one of them?"

"No, she had little to do with the deceased and she wasn't in a relationship, so there was no man for Mary to steal." I shrugged. Jules was always too busy shooting, mountain climbing or playing sport in the little time she had away from training greyhounds to go looking for Mr. Right. "The murderer definitely set Jules up."

After cleaning his plate, Fred wiped spaghetti sauce off his chin with the cuff of his shirt. "That makes our task so much easier, Kat. We're looking for someone who had a grudge against both Mary Parker *and* your friend, Jules." He grinned and I could see pieces of spaghetti caught up in his teeth. "That should narrow the field down for us when we go door-knocking tomorrow."

I stared at him, aghast. Everyone seemed to forget the elephant in the room–I was getting married on Saturday. No time to go knocking on doors. And even if I did decide to help Jules by asking around, I wouldn't take Freddy the octogenarian with me. At the speed he moved, it would likely take two days to get from one end of the street to the other.

"Oh, good," said the woman who used to be my Gran. "I'll make sandwiches and cookies to take with us."

7

I STOOD ON THE PORT ADELAIDE WHARF the following morning, alongside the river, and watched the colors of sunrise. Varying shades of red orange and gold reached out across the lightening sky like buds fast-forwarding to flowers that you see in those Nature shows on television.

Unlike most people, I love early mornings. Which is just as well–'cos rain, hail or shine, it's mandatory for greyhound trainers to climb out of bed at dawn, layer-up or down according to the weather, and stagger outside to work their dogs. But today, as I watched the sunrise transform the river into a kaleidoscope of color, I realized how wonderful my life really was.

Determined to enjoy our morning walk, I pushed aside all thoughts of dead bodies and the two Wrinkly Gumshoes intent on not only dragging me into another investigation but accompanying me with their walkers and canes. Instead, I smiled down at Erin, my best friend's eleven-year-old daughter, better known as Devils Spawn. She was currently dragging the toes of her two-hundred-dollar sneakers along the sturdy planks of the wharf, her bottom lip down near her shoes.

"What's up kid?"

"Why do I always have to take the *little* one?" she said glaring down at Tater who was straining on the end of his lead. I shook my head. Luckily, my cupcake Chihuahua who always pictured himself as a Doberman had no idea he was the 'little' dog Erin referred to. Happy to be out and about, he turned his head and grinned up at her, his dark eyes brimming with mischief. She ignored him. "I'll be, like, twelve next month. I am totally strong enough to handle greyhounds."

"Indeed you are," I said, still smiling, still hovering up there on

Cloud Nine–until the four GAP dogs in my charge, excited about their new surroundings, headed in four different directions at once and brought me back to Planet Earth with a jolt.

"This is totally child-abuse," Erin continued completely ignoring my predicament. "Like, my mother forced me out of bed in the dark and then like, when I get here, I'm made to walk a pipsqueak of a dog instead of a greyhound."

Hopping on one foot, I quickly untangled the leads wrapped around my legs before flicking a look of exasperation in Erin's direction.

She'd been grumbling and flicking her long Princess-hair over her shoulder ever since we'd unloaded the dogs from the trailer. Okay, she was a cute kid, I guess, but sometimes I couldn't work out why Tanya didn't put her up for auction and let her go to the highest bidder. "Tater needs someone who'll take special care of him today," I said forcing my voice to stay pleasant. "Don't forget, as my flower girl, you're in charge of walking Tater down the aisle on Saturday, so you need all the practice you can get. Plus, if your mum or I take him at the moment, he might get trodden on by the bigger dogs and then he'll get mad and might try to eat them. We don't want that, do we?"

She thought about this for a moment, flicked her long hair over her shoulder once again and sniffed. Gradually the bottom lip rose from the ground to navel height and she gave a condescending nod. "Okay. I s'pose."

I swallowed a grin and metaphorically patted myself on the back. Hey, I was quite proud of the way I'd handled that one. Maybe I'd make a good mum after all. Maybe Ben and I would have children one day and they'd be loving and kind and obedient, all due to my exceptional mothering. But when the pink iPhone came out of Erin's back pocket and she walked on, head down, not looking where she or Tater were going, I frowned.

Or maybe not.

I'd arranged for Tanya and Erin to meet me at the wharf so the six GAP dogs in my care could interact with the sounds and sights of the river and learn to relax in a completely different environment from the race track. However, when I tried to escape the house without Lucky, Tater and Yolo, informing them this trip was only for the dogs I was currently fostering, it didn't happen. If looks could fry your liver and rip out your heart, I'd be lying on a slab in the mortuary. So, as usual, they won the argument and insisted on riding in the back of my station wagon while the fostered greyhounds were relegated to the trailer.

"It was weird last night," I told Tanya as I watched a small tug guide a large boat four times its size along the Port River toward us. "After Ma helped Gran and Fred haul their bags up to my guest room, she took off like a frightened rabbit. Must have switched her phone off the moment she drove through my gateway because I haven't been able to get through to her since."

Tanya let out a hoot. "Guess it was a shock to discover her mother had a boyfriend."

"You're right. She couldn't cope with the antics of the two loved-up seniors at all. Kept staring at Gran like she was a doppelganger."

"So, what happened after your Ma left?"

"Gran cooked us a delicious meal and while we ate, she and Fred made arrangements to take me sleuthing later today. Then, while I washed the dishes, they huffed and puffed their way up the stairs to their bedroom. Together." I shrugged one shoulder. "I didn't see them again until just before I left for the wharf this morning when they were both exiting my bathroom."

"They were in the bathroom together?"

"What can I say? Gran's hair was all mussed up and Fred, dressed in a red satin dressing gown, carried a balloon full of water in one hand while he steered his walker with the other."

Tanya opened her mouth to speak, but I broke in. "Hey, don't ask me what they had in mind for the balloon. You're the sexpert around here. You tell me."

The tantalizing smells of grilled sausages and onion, fried eggs and bacon, and hamburgers, drifted across the wharf from the early-morning vendors who'd set up their breakfast vans nearby. My stomach rumbled, reminding me I hadn't eaten since last night's Spaghetti Bolognese. Every dog's nose twitched, while Lucky peered up at me, her large brown eyes pleading, as if to say: '*Please, Mum, can I have five dollars to go buy a sausage-and-onion sandwich*?'

Coming from the other direction, I spotted a familiar figure walking three fit-looking greyhounds, on leads. It was a fellow-trainer, Peter Findlay. I waved. "Looks like Pete walks his dogs along the wharf too," I said shortening the leads on my four eager canines." I flicked a quick glance across at Erin and shook my head. Instead of watching Tater, who was in the process of cocking his leg and watering one of the uprights on a wooden park bench, she was responding to several of her thousand and one social media friends. "Erin!" I said. "Keep Tater on a short lead. He doesn't know Peter's dogs and might get stroppy."

"And if you don't put that phone away I'll confiscate it for the rest of the day," added Tanya, also bringing Lucky and Yolo, plus the two Gap dogs, Greta and Butch, closer to her side.

Peter Findlay, a backyard trainer who only ever had up to four dogs in work at the same time, slowed down and stopped beside us. Rufus leapt forward ready to play with Peter's dogs. I pulled him back and shook a finger at him. "Behave yourself. Not everyone's out for a game like you."

"G'day, Kat. Tanya. Little Erin." Peter's shy smile was the nicest thing about him. His clothes, wrinkled and in need of a wash, bagged on his skeletal frame and his hair was in need of a good shampoo. After Peter's divorce came through a little over a month ago, the weight dropped off him, leaving him looking older and more haggard than a once-good-looking forty-six-year-old man ever should. The only thing that kept him going was his greyhounds.

Erin let out a loud sigh and flicked her hair. "I am *not* little," she said, her voice frostier than a winter morning. "I'm, like, *twelve* next month."

Peter raised one eyebrow at her, his smile refusing to slip. "And quite the young lady you're becoming too, I might add." He turned to Tanya and winked. "You'll be beating the boys off with a stick before long."

"Hi Pete. Beautiful morning for a walk." Tanya greeted him and then without waiting for a response, babbled on. "Hey, did you hear Mary Parker was murdered? Kat found her in the dumpster at the track yesterday."

No wonder Erin had a sassy tongue. Her mother suffered from foot and mouth disease.

Peter's smile shut down and he studied the ground as though the news of the world was written there on the rough cement of the Port Adelaide wharf. "Yeah. Saw it on the telly last night."

"So, were you one of Mary's conquests?" There she went again. Tanya and Fred would be a great act together. Not a filter between them.

"Tanya!" I said watching Peter's frown deepen. "You're embarrassing Peter."

"Just asking. Anyway, Peter's a guy. He doesn't mind talking about that sort of thing. Do you, Pete?"

Peter let out a half- laugh, half-snort. "Actually, I do. But look, I'll say one thing–if you can name a male trainer who wasn't one of Mary's conquests, I'll shout you to a slap-up meal at the pub, okay? I'm sorry Mary's dead, of course, but she had issues. Massive issues. She played with men's emotions and acted like it was…I don't know…a game of Monopoly to her." He whooshed out a breath and chewed on his bottom lip. "My guess is some poor guy couldn't take her cruelty any longer and snapped." His jaw tightened. "Because Mary Parker was a nasty contagious disease."

Holy catfish! If all of Mary's male conquests thought the same as Peter it would be a matter of, 'Eeny, Meeny, Miney, Mo, which rejected lover flew off the handle and laid her low?'

And here was me thinking the murderer was a woman…

There was something else my new partner-in-sleuthing, Fred, the retired detective, had suggested. To reveal the murderer, find someone who not only had a grudge against Mary–apparently *they* were a dime a dozen–but also a grudge against Jules. Because why else would they frame her?

"The police arrested Julia Cassidy and charged her with Mary's murder," I told Peter, closely scrutinizing his expression for any tell-tale signs of guilt.

"*Jules*?" The only expression on Peter's face was of shock and disbelief. Either he was innocent or his acting attributes could see him starring in the next James Bond movie. "But that makes no sense," he went on, anger turning his face red. "Julia Cassidy was one of the few people in the greyhound industry who had no beef with Mary. Why would the police arrest her?"

"Because Mary Parker was killed with Jules' gun."

He shook his head. "I don't believe it. Either someone stole her gun and framed her or the police have the wrong gun."

"I'm with you, Pete, but we need to help Jules prove her innocence," I said leaning into his face. "So, tell me, when was the last time you saw Julia Cassidy?"

"What do ya mean?" He frowned and backed away as though I'd suddenly sprouted an extra second head.

"Normal question. The police will want to know too–it's something they'll ask everyone associated with her."

"Oh. Right. Um…I guess the last time I saw Jules was three days ago, when I called in to use her hydro-bath on one of my dogs."

"Do you have any idea who'd want to get Jules in trouble?"

Peter slowly shook his head. "Can't imagine anyone hating Jules enough to implicate her in a murder. She's a good kid, straight as a die." He frowned. "Unless it's someone whose jealous because she's good at everything she does. But what would that have to do with Mary's murder?"

"Beats me," said Tanya. "But Jules is locked up in jail while the real murderer is still out here, acting like a normal person. And we need to do something about that."

Peter shrugged. "I'm all for helping Jules. But what can I do?"

"Just keep your eyes and ears open and if you hear anything interesting, report to Kat. She'll take it from there, okay?"

"Me?" First Gran and Fred twisting my arm to investigate and now Tanya. "In case you've forgotten, Tan, it's my wedding day on Saturday. I love Jules like a sister–but there's nothing I can do. In two days' time, Ben and I are getting married and then we're off to Kangaroo Island for our honeymoon."

"All the more reason to wrap this up quickly by asking questions and demanding answers. Jules needs you, Kat."

By this time the GAP dogs, plus Lucky and Yolo, had lost interest in the surroundings and were all stretched out on the wharf asleep, little Petunia with her head resting on Rufus's stomach. However, I could see Tater eyeing off Peter's four racing greyhounds as though he wanted to take them all on at once. They were completely ignoring him, but that didn't stop the feisty Chihuahua's hackles from rising as he scratched the ground and glared up at them.

Time to move on. Especially as Erin's eyes and attention, instead of being on her tiny charge, were centered on a brightly colored ice cream van parked over near the Port Lighthouse. While we'd been talking, the owner of the van had set up a colorful sign listing all the different flavors he had available.

Saying goodbye to Peter who seemed intent on walking his team the full-length of the wharf and back, we headed to the side street where we'd parked our vehicles. I had a busy day ahead of me and so did Tanya. After dropping her almost-twelve-year-old, incorrigible daughter off at school, she then had a full day at *The Luv Bug*.

"Well," said Tanya, "what did you make of Peter?"

"You mean, other than the fact his hair is about two weeks overdue for a shampoo and his sneakers are ingrained with dirt?"

"And did you see his sweater? If he wears that brown sweater one more day, it'll stand up and walk itself to the washing machine. But no,

I meant what did you make of his answers? He admitted he had a pretty hot motive for killing Mary?"

"As do ninety percent of the other male trainers," I said as Rufus attempted to investigate a cheesy smell coming from a trash can as we passed. I gave a small tug on his lead to discourage his interest. "You heard him. Peter has no beef with Jules. She's his friend, so why would he frame her?"

"You're so naïve at times, Kat. Haven't you heard that old saying, 'Methinks he doth protest too much'? Well, that's what it sounded like to me. Peter had a motive. He hated Mary's guts. And I know for a fact, he often called into Jules' to use her hydro-bath, or slip dogs up her straight track because living in suburbia, he has access to neither. How easy would it be for him to sneak into the house and steal two guns while Jules was busy with her own dogs?"

Reaching the dog trailer, I opened the doors so each dog could jump in. "But was Peter at Jules' property yesterday morning? That's when she discovered the guns were missing."

"Maybe they were stolen earlier than that. Maybe Jules only found the guns were gone when she went looking for them yesterday morning."

I let out a sigh. There were so many maybes to this case. Maybe I needed to use my charm on DI Adams. Buy him e-cigarettes in exchange for looking the other way while I asked Jules a few pertinent questions.

Or maybe Gran could threaten more finger breaking to coerce Uncle Tony into asking the questions for me.

8

THEY WERE WAITING FOR ME. Like bad smells after eating baked beans. They were waiting for me.

The moment I opened the gate and drove the car down the driveway they burst through the front door, calling and waving their arms to attract my attention. Pretzel-shaped Fred, pushing his walker in front of him and Gran, dressed in old lady's clothes and loaded down with a basket of goodies as if we were setting out on a Sunday school picnic.

I returned their wave but didn't slow down. First there were GAP dogs to unload and feed plus Ben and Jake might need a hand. With Ben's team of dogs housed in the newly built kennel house across from mine, we now had 25 racing dogs to work each morning. I let out a sigh. Hopefully the guys could manage without me for a while longer as my grandmother and her ex-detective beau were anxious to get going. It was almost like they'd been waiting on the other side of the front door listening for the crunch of my car wheels on the gravel driveway.

"What's with your new roomies?" asked Ben on his way back from grading the dog runs. Legs apart, he halted in front of the kennel house, his hair tousled like a little boy, but the snug tee-shirt that caressed his chest muscles proving he was neither little, nor a boy.

"We're door knocking," I told him as I let each dog out of the trailer and watched them scamper through the open doorway of the new building.

"Why? Collecting for charity?"

I rolled my eyes. "You don't want to know." I opened the back door of the station wagon and moved to the side to let Lucky, Tater and Yolo follow the other dogs into the granny flat. "Sorry Ben, can't stop. The early morning river air has turned the multitude into starving strays."

Collecting eight dog dishes from the cupboard under the sink–may as well feed my three at the same time – I spread the dishes on the kitchen table and then stepped between dogs to walk across to the fridge. Eight bowls of Weetabix coming up. As I bent over to snaffle two large cartons of milk from the bottom shelf, a strong arm wrapped itself around my middle and tugged me backwards until I hit the rock-hard chest of one slightly pissed off fiancé. "But I do want to know," was all he said, his warm breath waking all the erogenous zones on the back of my neck. "And if it's at all dangerous you can wait until the racing dogs are finished and I'll come with you."

I turned around and slung both arms around Ben's neck, linked my fingers and tugged his head down so his mouth was lined up with mine. "Thanks, but I already have more protection than I can cope with. In fact, it's The Gran and Freddikens Show–not mine." I rolled my eyes. "Think I'm little more than their getaway driver."

His laugh was warm as he closed the distance between our lips. "That's what I love about you, babe, you're never boring."

"Glad to be of assistance," I said, my hands leaving his neck and slipping under his tee-shirt to tug him closer. I closed my eyes and let my fingers spread wider, kneading, enjoying the texture of his strong masculine physique. Mine. All mine. If we were alone, his tee-shirt, along with those yummy butt-hugging jeans would be on the floor and the little bed in the room at the back of the granny flat christened. But with eight dogs underfoot and noisily demanding breakfast, the racing team to be worked and fed and two impatient senior citizens hovering around outside, we settled for a long lingering kiss.

"How many more days?" he moaned as we came up for air

"Just over two."

"And then we'll be in a plane and heading for the bridal suite at a posh B&B in Kangaroo Island for seven sex-packed days." That wicked grin I'd come to love spread across his face as he kissed me on the tip of my nose. "I can't wait."

And neither could I.

"Yoo! Hoo!"

I turned my head to find my Gran leaning against the door jamb. She was wearing one of her famous vinegar faces. "Come along, Katrina. We have work to do and no time to waste on frivolous smooching."

"Frivolous?" My voice shot up an octave. "Ben's my fiancé."

She harrumphed. "Maybe, but if we're to get this investigation on the road and locate a witness who saw someone suspicious hanging around your friend, Jules' house on the day her guns were stolen, we have no time for smooching."

"Okay. Point taken. I'll be ready to leave as soon as I've fed these dogs."

"I'm sorry to sound like a killjoy, dear, but with you and Whatshisname all set to take off for your honeymoon on Saturday, our time is limited." She pursed her lips. "Unless you cancel your honeymoon, of course."

Cancel our honeymoon? I blinked in confusion and heard Whatshisname let out a snort of disbelief behind me.

Head cocked to one side, she eyed us off, one eyebrow raised in query. "Oh well," she said with a final fatalistic shrug, "We'll just have to pull on our gum-shoes and crack this case before the wedding then. No time to lose."

Was this woman really my Granny Hamilton? The clothes were the same. The way her hair was set in an iron tight perm was the same. But the words coming from this woman's mouth were so far removed from the straight-laced grandmother I'd been afraid of all my life, I couldn't be sure.

"Wait out in the car, Gran. I'll be there soon."

I quickly shook the Weetabix box over the eight bowls and added milk then set them apart from each other in a row on the floor. "Do you mind taking my three dogs back to the house when they're finished?" I asked Ben, leaning forward for another quick kiss. "Otherwise, someone I thought I knew might have a heart attack from stressing out while waiting in the car," I added in a whisper.

"Sure. But I want you to promise not to do anything stupid while you're out knocking on doors with your fellow sleuths. Right?"

"Stupid? Like what?"

"Like enter a house if you don't know the person who invited you in–like climb through a window if there's no one home–like annoy the home-owner enough for them to call the police…" He cocked one eyebrow. "Shall I go on?"

"Okay, Dad, I'll be careful," I said and dodging when he made a grab at me, I scuttled out the door.

Fred had already made himself at home in the back of my car. In fact, he'd taken over the entire back seat with his walker, an oversized pair of sunglasses, a tin of toffees and what looked like an unopened packet of bullets. Swallowing a scream, I scowled down at him. "Don't tell me you've brought a gun?"

"Okay, Kitty-Kat," he said his voice sing-song and his grin widening. "I won't tell you I've brought a gun."

"I don't believe this!" I closed my eyes and tried to think of happy things like little fairy dolls and baby rattles but all I could come up with was a bloody great hole in the fairy doll's stomach. "This is so not happening to me!"

I shook my head. What had I ever done to deserve this? Not only did I have to look after my grandmother and her new lover while investigating a murder and answer to my mother if either of them ended up in hospital, now I had to worry about where Fred had stashed his gun. And no way was I digging into his old man clothes to locate it.

"Don't worry, Kat," Fred said, eyes twinkling beneath his thick snowy white eyebrows. "You can stop hyperventilating. It's only a toy gun–but looks extremely life-like. Even an expert would have trouble distinguishing it from the real thing in a line up.”

I whooshed out a sigh of relief and climbed into the car. The sooner I took Fred and Gran on their little expedition and returned them safe and sound to the front door of my house, the sooner I could relax.

Fred continued to spout his police know-how from the seat behind me. “One of the first lessons you learn when you become a detective is–always look pro-active in the company of bad guys. I found early on that a gun in the hand is worth more than a thousand words.”

“Hmm…” I said, going along with his philosophy while praying we had no need to confront any bad guys–toy gun or not–while door knocking this morning. “I can see how that would work.”

“Do you have a notebook and pencil in your pocket for when we question our perps?”

“Nope.” I leant across Gran and her basket of goodies, plucked my iPad from the car’s glove box and switched it on. “We modern detectives use tablets instead of notebooks now.” I passed the tablet over to him. “Instead of planning how to use that toy gun on imaginary bad guys, why not keep your mind occupied with some word games while we’re driving to Jules’ house. Quite a few apps to choose from, but Scrabble, Wheel of Fortune and Crossword Classic should keep you out of trouble.”

“Hmm…I’m rather good at solving crosswords,” he said removing a pair of glasses from his inside pocket and studying the screen.

“Go on then Fred, knock yourself out.”

Jules lived a ten-minute drive away on Short Rd., an area that housed mostly families living on from two to ten acre blocks. Not what my two assistants were expecting, however. As I turned the corner and drove past three properties, slowing down in front of Jules’ house, I noticed the look of confusion on Gran’s face. Being a suburbanite all her life, I guess she was expecting a row of units or small residential homes and didn’t realize what door knocking in the country actually entailed.

“We’ll leave our car in Jules’ driveway and work our way out from there," I said parking the station wagon in front of Jules' two-bedroom transportable home. Although Jules lived in a modest house, her kennel block was made of brick, the long runs were constructed of quality steel posts and heavy-duty wire, and she had every mod con imaginable for the dogs. Even the large shed where she practiced her shooting was new and shiny.

There were no dogs on the property. After Jules desperate phone call the day before, Ben drove straight around with his trailer and collected her ten race dogs. We'd kept two and distributed the rest among fellow trainers. It was just the done thing. In the greyhound world dogs always came first and where possible trainers helped each other out when in trouble.

Even if the trainer had been accused of murder.

With difficulty, I extracted Fred from the bowels of the back seat. I set him on his feet, hat on head, hands on walker, two toffees in each pocket and a warning to keep his gun well-hidden as we didn't want someone ringing the police and causing a fiasco. Then, turning to Ma, I wrestled the basket from her claw-like fingers and returned it to the front seat of the car, promising we'd come back in an hour and have our picnic. I even pulled three bottles of water from the basket and shoved one in each of our pockets.

"When did you get so bossy?" Gran snapped as I relieved her of a bag of cookies and returned it to the basket for the third time.

"Pot. Kettle. Black," I muttered through gritted teeth, my head inside the car.

"You were always such a chicken of a kid when you were younger. I could always make you cry, just by looking at you."

"I'm not five any more, Gran." Giving her the evil eye, I pulled up my big girl pants and led them through the gate onto the property next door. "We'll start here. If anyone in the street is in a position to notice suspicious goings-on, it will surely be Jules' next-door neighbors."

On the way to the front door, we counted five discarded bikes of various sizes, some with one wheel, a couple with no wheels. These lay in the dirt next to headless dolls, broken toy trucks, saggy cardboard boxes and other junk, including several rusty coffee tins filled with dried-out dirt and dying plants. With each step we took, Gran's mouth set more firmly in a straight line. By the time we reached the sagging front verandah, she looked ready to rip strips off the householder with her bare tongue.

"Not a word," I told her as I kicked a dead rat off the mat and knocked on the front door. "We want the resident to answer our questions, not swing a punch at you in defense of their rights."

"Vee," said Fred touching Gran on the arm. "Behave yourself. We're amateur detectives–not Tidy-Town judges."

I could see Gran's cock sparrow demeanor slowly deflate like a perished balloon. "People like this should be fined for polluting the planet," she grumbled glaring down at the unfortunate rat whose bedraggled and bloody appearance made me think he'd recently been part of a dog's dinner.

There was no sign of anyone becoming at all interested in discovering who was knocking at their front door. And it wasn't as if they didn't know we were there. The pack of dogs inside the house were making enough noise to wake up Rip Van Winkle.

I knocked again, louder. But all this did was infuriate the doggy residents of the house even further. The way they were slamming their bodies against the front door made me take a couple of steps back and study the rusty hinges which seemed to be getting looser with each body-slam.

Fred, a little shaken, gripped his walker with unsteady hands. "Shall we try around the back?" he said in a voice that indicated he'd rather jump into shark infested waters, if that was another option.

"Not much point," I said and watched both Fred and Gran nod in quick agreement. "The dogs have let their owners know we're here so I guess they don't want to talk to us. Let's try the next property on our list."

Leaving the mad dogs to eventually smash through the vulnerable door without us, we scrambled through the front gate, quickly latched it behind us, and then, after Gran and Fred leant against the fence for a few moments to regain their breath, shuffled off past Jules' house to No. 64, the property on the other side. Although I'd driven past and admired this place from the car when visiting Jules, I'd never been inside the front gate. Compared to The Planet of the Ferocious Dogs, No. 64 was like one of those immaculately set-up country estates in England. I could see two magnificent mares with their spindly legged foals grazing contentedly in an irrigated paddock just inside gate. A deep sandy lunging arena a little further on. And a newly-raked pebbled path which led to the rear of the property, where a house, big enough to accommodate three families and a team of servants, sat smugly surrounded by lawns and landscaped flower beds.

"Chalk and cheese," I said, eying off the estate.

"Wouldn't be surprised if a butler answered the front door," Gran agreed.

To the right, I could see four brick stables with metal yards attached and a full-sized dressage arena where a woman in well-fitting jodhpurs and long black boots, her hair tied back in a neat ponytail, rode a stunning chestnut horse. Both horse and rider were concentrating on the movements they were performing. The horse, although large and muscly, was so light on its feet it appeared to be dancing as the rider asked him to side-pass across the arena and then come to a square halt. She sat straight-backed in the saddle watching us walk toward her.

"Can I help you?" she asked, her voice a little brittle as though annoyed that we'd disturbed her concentration.

I stepped into the arena and reached up to pat the magnificent chestnut on the neck. "I don't know if you've heard, but your neighbor, Jules Cassidy is in jail. She's been accused of a crime she didn't commit and we were wondering if you could help us prove her innocence."

The woman shook her head. "Sorry, I know nothing about the woman who lives next door, other than she continually scares our horses with those guns of hers. In fact, we've even been to the council and the police in an effort to stop her. She's dangerous."

I looked around at the stables, the dressage arena, the expensive double float parked in a garage next to the stable and frowned. "I'm guessing your passion is training and competing in dressage?"

She nodded. "I think that's pretty obvious."

"Well, can't you see how passionate Jules is with her target-shooting? That's what makes her tick. She works her butt off practicing at home, and then competes against the best in her rank. Next month she'll be trying out against other Australians to represent her country at the Commonwealth Games." A flicker of interest sparked in the woman's eyes. "So, you of all people, should understand where Jules is coming from when she practices all hours of the day. She's as dedicated to her sport as you are to yours."

She shrugged one shoulder. "Okay, what do you want to know?"

Gran took a hesitant step forward, keeping plenty of open space between her and the large horse. She waved one arm in the direction of Jules's property. "Well, have you noticed anything suspicious going on next door?"

"Other than guns going off at all hours of the day or night, define suspicious."

"I don't know, do I, young lady?" Gran drew herself up and sent the woman one of her iciest glares. "That's why I'm asking you."

Fred and I exchanged a quick eye roll, silently agreeing Gran lacked the subtlety to ever become a successful sleuth. Then, with a warning nudge to zip her lips, Fred pushed past Gran and trundled his walker a little closer to the arena

"It's like this, dear," Fred said as he flashed his fangs at the woman on the horse. "Have you noticed anyone sneaking around Jules' property? Breaking into her house? Parking out the front for an extended period of time? Anything at all? Even the smallest crumb of information might help to prove her innocence."

The woman frowned and then slowly shook her head. "Look, I really can't help you. When I'm out here with my horses I'm in another world.

I don't know what's going on around me. It's only when I hear gunshots that I even look across the fence at my neighbor's property." She did the delicate shoulder shrug thing again. "Sorry."

"That's okay, dear. You have a good day." Fred maneuvered his walker around to face the opposite direction in readiness to leave. "And good luck with your dressage."

I turned with Fred and hooked my arm through Gran's. Seemed like our door knocking expedition was proving to be a waste of time–something I had little of to spare.

"Hang on, there was that pizza delivery guy the night before last…"

We all spun around so quickly, Fred almost toppled over. If Gran and I hadn't grabbed him he'd have gone splat on the newly raked gravel. "What Pizza delivery guy?"

"He knocked on our door and asked if the woman from number 62 was with us. He said she'd rung in an order but wasn't home and did I know where she was, or if he'd mistaken the number and we'd ordered the pizza."

"And?" I said, wondering where this was going.

"And nothing." From high on her horse she looked down her nose at me. "I told the guy hell would freeze over before I ate pizza–they're for peasants and the chronically obese–and the woman from next door would never be welcome at No. 64. Then I shut the door on him." She used her legs to give an aide to her horse, asking him to turn and walk on.

I scowled at her back. "Well, can you at least remember the name on the pizza delivery vehicle?"

As she and the horse continued toward the other side of the arena she called out over her shoulder. "It was the local shop, Two Wells Pizzas. Only ones who deliver out here."

I banged myself upside the head. Of course, I should have known. Every Friday night I had a large pizza-with-the-lot delivered to my front door from that very shop.

"A pizza delivery to an empty house?" Puzzled, I turned away and led my two unlikely assistants back to the front gate. "What do you make of that?"

"I suppose Jules could have rung in the order and then been called out on an emergency."

Gran's explanation made sense. "True," I said, "but wouldn't she ring and cancel the order?"

"Not if it was an emergency."

"Okay, but what if someone else rang the order through and parked outside, waiting to see if Jules answered the door when the pizza delivery guy knocked. You know, to make sure she wasn't home before breaking in and stealing the murder weapon."

"Hmm…" said Fred, puffing a little as he leaned against the fence while I closed and latched the gate on No. 64. "It does seem rather fishy."

Gran nodded. "Another question for Tony to put to his client."

"Or maybe a simple phone call to Two Wells Pizza shop might jog the delivery boy's memory," I added.

9

Still discussing our one and only clue–a pizza delivery ordered from an empty house–Gran, Fred and I trundled slowly across the road to the house opposite. No. 63. Okay, it wasn't much of a clue, but at least it was somewhere to start.

The two elderly sleuths looked to be tiring, especially Fred, whose liver-spotted hands were a little shaky as he gripped the handle of his walker. If there were no more clues to be found at No. 63 it might be time to quit–or at least retire to the car and enjoy the contents of Gran's bulging picnic basket. My ever-eager stomach rumbled at the thought. The smell of hot roast chicken emanating from the depths of that basket had teased my taste buds all the way from home.

Meanwhile, before tackling the residents of No. 63, I called for a five-minute breather. Immediately Fred locked his walker in place and collapsed onto the padded seat, while Gran, after stretching her fingers several times, stepped behind the walker and began to give him a shoulder massage. A massage that soon had him purring more like a tiger than a domestic cat. Smiling at this scene of domestic bliss, I turned my back on them and decided to check out our one and only clue. The pizza delivery.

As Two Wells Pizza was already on my speed dial, the moment I clicked on my phone, I got straight onto Johnny, the proprietor. And, as usual, he wanted to discuss the winning chances of the race dogs we had entered at Angle Park that night–Johnny was a mad punter–but as soon as that was out the way, I asked if I could speak to the delivery boy who'd found no one home at Jules' house on Tuesday night.

"Hang on, Kat, I'll get Luke for you."

A cocky-voiced adolescent came on the phone. "Yeah?"

"Hi Luke, sorry to bother you, but I need to ask you a few questions." Silence on the other end, so I continued. "Firstly, can you remember if there was a car parked out the front of Julia Cassidy's house when you drove into her driveway Tuesday night?"

"Nah."

"Nah, you can't remember or Nah, there was no car?"

"Nah, I wasn't looking."

I chewed on my bottom lip and told myself I was once a cocky teenager myself. If I jumped down his throat he'd only put up a sulky brick wall. "Luke, this is important. It's a murder enquiry. Now, if you don't answer *my* questions you could have the police knocking on your door and you never know what they might find hidden in your underwear drawer while they're poking around."

"Okay, okay, don't get ya thong in a twist, lady. Johnny only pays us like when we collect from the customer, so when the bird didn't answer the front door, I went around the back and knocked again. Still no answer. Wasted trip. Felt like kicking her puny pot plants over."

"And this is leading where?"

"Well, while I was like, round the back, I did see a car parked behind some bushes. Didn't take much notice at the time. Thought it belonged to the customer."

"Okay, Luke, that's good. Now, can you tell me the make of the car, or if there was anyone sitting inside?"

"Nah. Too dark."

"Can you at least tell me the color of the car?"

"Um…darkish. I think. Hey, I wasn't looking, was I? Just wanted me money. Even went next door. Thought I might be able to offload the pizza there but the bird was so up herself like her nose was–"

"Okay, I get the picture," I said. "And you didn't see anyone lurking around either house?"

"Nah. Already told ya that."

We were back where we started and it seemed like I wouldn't get any more from Cocky Teenager, so I thanked him and ended the call.

A darkish car–maybe–parked behind some bushes around the back. Not much to go on.

By this time Gran's massage had slipped from the shoulders to further down Fred's body, so I shoved the phone back in my pocket, called the lovebirds to order, waited until Fred was back on his feet and then opened the gate of No. 63.

Once inside, we were confronted by a neat transportable timber-framed home which sat slap-bang in the center of a rather rundown property. As though the resident was either unable to use his lawn mower or it had broken down a year ago and he hadn't bothered replacing it.

I cast a wary eye around. No dogs in sight–fierce or otherwise–only a goat and a scruffy black sheep, both munching on an open bale of hay over by the side fence. Fred, evidently energized from his massage, elbowed his way to the front of our little threesome, almost taking a chunk out of the back of my leg with his walker in his enthusiasm. And then, ignoring my yelps of pain, clambered up onto the verandah in front of me. "Let *me* do the talking this time," he told us as he straightened his blue and white striped bow tie before fixing a shark-like smile on his face. "People sometimes underestimate old people and tend to drop their guard."

"Have at it," I said, stepping back and rubbing at the likely bruise on the back of my left calf. He could be right though. Sometimes people *did* underestimate old people–especially when they used their mobility aids as weapons.

Squaring his bird-like shoulders Fred winked at Gran and then banged determinedly on the door with one gnarled fist.

Immediately there was a shuffling noise, like someone moving very slowly inside the house. We waited. And waited. Until, several minutes later, the front door creaked open about eighteen inches, to reveal what looked like a shriveled-up pixie leaning heavily on two walking sticks, one for each hand. The shriveled-up old man wore tired brown slippers, ancient suit pants and the front of his shabby grey cardigan was covered in crumbs.

Fred, taken aback, blinked rapidly. The man standing hunched up in the doorway had to be over a hundred–or at least a badly-worn 98.

I grinned at Fred. So much for having an advantage due to his age.

The white-haired centenarian peered at us through rheumy eyes. "Stone the flamin' crows, what have we here?" he croaked in a voice that had gone rusty with over-use. "Not selling religion, are ya? If so, I reckon it might be a bit late for me."

Gran was the first to recover. "Good morning, sir," she said, patting at her head-hugging perm and giving the man a very un-Granny-like smile, causing Fred to growl deep in his throat like a jealous bull striking at the ground, ready to cross horns in a duel for his lady. "I'm Mrs. Hamilton. This young fellow here is ex-Detective Fred Turner. And the child biting her nails is my granddaughter, Katrina. We're here because the young lady over the road from you has been wrongly accused of murder and we were wondering if you would be kind enough to help us by answering a few questions."

"Strewth!" the pixie yelled as he made an adjustment to his hearing aid. "Has that gal over the road gone and shot someone with one of those flamin' guns she uses to take pot-shots at tins and bottles? Fair dinkum, I reckon she's got a few kangaroos loose in her top paddock–if you know what I mean."

Gran's eyes widened. "What? She shoots at kangaroos? But that's–"

"No, no," said Fred. "He means she's not all there. She's a little loco."

"Oh." Gran, evidently not invested in Aussie slang, stepped back to allow one of us to continue the questioning.

"Well, come on, whatcha wanna know? I'm a ticking time bomb, ya know. Every breath could be my last."

I stepped forward. "Sir, can you remember seeing anyone acting suspiciously around Jules' property yesterday morning–or even the night before? You see, the real killer stole two of my friend's guns and used one to shoot another woman. And the police, idiots that they are, arrested Jules for a crime she didn't commit. So…if you could help us, we'd be really indebted to you."

"Goodo," he said and nodded at me. His pink scalp peeping through the thin white hair bobbed up and down with each nod. "Now, let me think." Frowning, he took out his top plate and dug what could have been a piece of oatmeal from breakfast, or even a remnant from last night's meal from between two of the front teeth, then carefully returned the denture to his mouth. "Ya know, I did see a bloke over there early yesterday morning. I was out here having a Captain's Cook at what those blasted galahs were up to. Bloody birds strip me trees of bark they do. Should get that gal to come over and shoot them for me. Anyway…this bloke, dunno his name, but he's always hanging around the place with his greyhounds, pulled up down the road a bit and walked to the lass's place. Thought that was a bit strange, like. I mean, why didn't he park in her driveway?"

"What time was this?" asked Fred.

"Hey, fair shake of the sauce bottle, mate, I've been retired for nearly forty years now. Only clock I live by is me worn-out body clock. What happened, see, I had to get up to go water the snake and saw the sun coming up, so I goes shuffling out to the front yard to chuck rocks at the bloody galas, and that's when I saw him."

I leaned forward. "Can you describe this guy?"

"Aaah…can't see too good these days." The old man scratched at his ear. "But I do remember the car. It was a green van. I've seen this bloke at the lass's place before. Usually pulls a dog trailer behind the van, but he didn't have the trailer on that morning."

"Anyone you know with a green van, Kat?" Fred turned to me.

I frowned. "Peter Findlay has a green van and he's often at Jules' with his dogs. He uses her straight track and hydro-bath."

I could feel my skin going cold and clammy. If it was Peter, why was he sneaking around Jules' property at daybreak before she was out of bed? And why did he tell me he hadn't seen her on the day of Mary Parker's murder?

Did he steal Jules' guns?

And did he use one of the stolen guns to shoot the woman who'd led him on and then betrayed him? The woman he'd left his wife and kids for? Mary Parker?

My stomach rumbled and performed a half-assed somersault, but this time it wasn't due to the smell of roast chicken. More like the smell of fear.

Did I really want to follow this clue and pay Peter Findlay a visit?

10

My heart skipped a beat. There were two motorbikes parked in front of the granny-flat housing the current batch of GAP dogs. Or to be more precise, two beautiful big black and chrome Harleys, so shiny I had to squint and reach in the car's console for my sunglasses. Even from a distance I spotted the pink sleeping bag protruding from the luggage strapped to the back of one. A Cheshire cat grin split my face. I'd know that sleeping bag anywhere.

Scuzz and Thunder had arrived.

I stopped in front of the house and in a tangle of arms and legs threw myself out of the car and onto the driveway. Yay! Scuzz and his half-sister, Thunder had arrived a day early. They were here. In the granny flat. Waiting for me.

I stuck my head through the open window of the car. "Will you be two be okay to get yourselves inside?"

"Humph!" said Gran, opening the passenger door and swiveling her sensibly-shod feet out onto the gravel. "We're not helpless, you know, Katrina. On a good day I can still touch my toes."

"Yeah," put in Fred from the back seat. "And on a good day, when the stars are all aligned and the wind's blowing the right way, I can still touch my knees…sometimes."

"Okay. I'll be back soon to let Tater and the two girls out."

Gran sent me another dragon-scowl. "I said we're not helpless,

Katrina. The day neither Fred nor I can open the back door and let three dogs out in the yard is the day we visit the undertaker to order our coffins. Now, go, see your friends."

"Thanks, Gran." I bent and kissed the top of her iron grey perm then, giving Fred a finger wave, took off running toward the kennel area.

"Scuzz! Thunder! Where are you?"

My two biker friends were here for the wedding. They'd also offered to stay in the granny-flat so they could look after the GAP dogs and help Jake with the racing team while Ben and I were on our honeymoon.

As I approached, a giant of a man dressed head to toe in black leather, appeared at the doorway of the granny-flat. The emblem on his jacket declared him to be a Red Dragon and the size of his hands and feet declared he could squash bad guys with one leisurely realignment of his massive shoulders. I watched him duck his head to fit under the doorway. Scuzz, or Theodore Samuel Parkington the Third–the name written on his birth certificate – was a fearsome warrior whose piercing black eyes could scare the scales off a crocodile. Yet when he returned my grin, they were softer than the pink sleeping bag he flaunted in his luggage. Three of the GAP greyhounds, gazing up at him with adoration, were tangled up in his legs, each one vying for the big guy's attention.

"Katrina, you're looking more gorgeous every time I see you," he said in that posh private-school voice that always warmed my insides. "Come here and give me a hug."

I threw myself into his arms, breathing in his distinctive smell of engine oil and expensive citrus-scented cologne. "It's so good to see you, Scuzz. But, hey, I didn't expect you until tomorrow."

"We decided to leave a day early and surprise you," a laughing voice called out from behind the hulk. It was Thunder, also dressed in black leather, right down to her long black boots. "Big brother couldn't wait a day longer to see you."

"Well, Big Brother had better do his looking from a distance. Like a hundred yards at all times." Ben stalked out of the kennel house and stood, hands on hips, eyes blazing up at the seven foot giant. A lot like the day Scuzz taunted him into proposing to me out on the open driveway, instead of the intimacy of the bedroom.

"Good afternoon, Benjamin. Been looking after my girl for me while I've been away?"

"Aaarrrgggh!"

"You know, I still have a couple of days left to change Katrina's mind," he said sending me a mischievous wink. "Personally, I can't see how she could prefer a skinny guy like you over an amazing individual like me." With his arms wrapped around me, Scuzz spoke to Ben over the top of my head which was snuggled into to the soft leather of his jacket.

I smothered a laugh. These two men were good mates but when I was around, you'd never know it. "Scuzz, behave yourself." I pulled back, looked up into those two black twinkling eyes and decided it was time to change the subject. "You and Thunder all set to play with the GAP dogs while Ben and I are away?"

"I think our biggest problem will be finding room on our beds for them at night." Thunder looked up from her position down on one knee as she tickled Petunia's stomach. The little white and black girl lay on her back, four legs in the air and an expression of pure bliss on her face.

"We can't thank you guys enough," I said inhaling the biker's wonderful citrus smell before moving across to Ben who smelt of sweat and wet dog. He must have been hydro-bathing some of the youngsters while I was off sleuthing with the oldies.

"Yes, mate. Thanks." As I drew closer, Ben's arm snaked out like a lasso and yanked me up against him. "And you too, Thunder. Just knowing you're both here to help Jake out with the racing dogs as well as the Gappies will give us peace of mind." Ben pulled me so close to him a cigarette paper would have battled to force its way between us. "Means Kat and I can completely relax and enjoy each other." He glared at Scuzz. "On our honeymoon."

This possessiveness might be sweet but Ben's grip was so tight the blood had banked up in my arms and was battling to flow through to my fingers. "Let me go, Ben," I said, attempting to shake him off. "I have a ring on my finger to show ownership and will be saying I do on Saturday, so there's no need to clamp me in irons until then. I'm yours. I love you. Okay?"

Ben's grip loosened and that sexy grin that always turned me on spread across his face. "Okay, babe. Sorry. Although…the thought of you handcuffed to my bed, completely at my mercy, while I…"

"Enough!" I yelled and felt my cheeks go hot. Both with embarrassment and the way my legs wobbled as this picture crystalized in my mind.

"Can we play that game on our honeymoon? Pretty please?"

"Thunder, is there anything you need for your stay in the granny-flat?" I said ignoring Ben's question although I'd be quite willing to discuss the matter later. Like two minutes after we arrived in the Bridal Suite at the Kangaroo Island resort.

"We're good." Thunder stood up, ran a hand through her long hair. "We packed the bare essentials on the bike but the rest of our luggage will be arriving by courier later today. Quite a nice little set-up you have in here. All I really need to do is go food shopping."

Food shopping!

Oh my God, the shopping list Gran gave me last night was still screwed up in the back pocket of my jeans. "Tell you what," I said, "give me an hour to catch up on some office-work and then I'll drive you to the nearest shopping center. I need food too."

"Deal."

After spending an hour on the computer, checking bank accounts, studying feature races scheduled for the next couple of months, writing up all medications and treatments carried out on our racing dogs over the last week into the official Treatment Book and filing anything tax-related–something Ben always left to me–I logged off and made my way outside, stretching and rolling the kinks out of both shoulders.

Ben's van was parked outside the kennel house and he was busy loading four bouncing greyhounds into the trailer. He looked across and grinned. "Finished the books?"

I nodded.

"Okay, I'm off to trial the youngsters now. Should be home by the time you and Thunder return from shopping."

I stood and watched him. Ben was always so patient with the dogs. He'd make a great dad if we ever decided to replace puppies for human babies. Three of the dogs were already in the trailer, but the last one, a gangly fawn pup, was spinning and leaping in the air, his high-pitched bark piercing my eardrums. He'd evidently spotted the stray cat that lived in our woodpile and thrived on mice, lizards and teasing my dogs. I'd have shouted at him, but Ben merely hung onto the dog's lead and waited for the cat to stride past with his tail high in the air, ignoring both humans and canines. Then, once the cat disappeared into the woodpile, Ben spoke calmly, waited for the dog to respond and when he finally jumped into the trailer with his mates, scratched him behind the ears

How could I not love this man?

"Any problems on your door-knocking expedition this morning?" Ben asked as he climbed into his van and fastened his seat belt.

I grinned as I wandered across to the driver's side window. "You mean, other than from the two pensioners who accompanied me?"

"Disastrous was it?"

"Nah. Not really. I think Gran and Fred had a blast." My grin widened. "And I guess it'll be even more fun for them when they return to Resthaven. Think of the embellished stories they'll have to share with the other residents."

Ben grinned. "I'd like to be a fly on the wall when that happens."

"I have a strong suspicion our two superheroes toddled straight on up to the bedroom after I dropped them at the front door."

Ben wagged his eyebrows. "The bedroom?"

I punched him on the arm. This guy had a one track mind. "Not for hanky-panky, Benjamin. But for a much-needed afternoon nap."

"Well, I don't need an afternoon nap." He wiggled his eyebrows again and leaned his head out the window for a kiss.

I obliged and would have probably made him late for the trials if a husky voice behind me hadn't dragged me away from those oh-so-hot lips.

"Yo!" It was my kennel-assistant, Jake. Who else would use, Yo! as a greeting? Obviously so accustomed to seeing us with our lips melded the dreadlocked hippie didn't think twice about breaking us up. "Okay if I, like, go home for lunch now, dudes?"

I unplugged my lips, nodded at Jake and then stepped away from temptation. We had two dogs racing at Angle Park tonight which meant we'd be leaving for the track in two and half hours. If I didn't take Thunder shopping now, I'd have to put it off until tomorrow and there was so much to fit into tomorrow, including a Hen's night with the girls.

"Hey, Thunder?" I called out, poking my head through the front doorway of the Granny flat. "You ready?"

She strolled from the bedroom into the kitchen, hair tidied and pulled back with a rubber band, more make-up applied, but except for exchanging her long black boots for black flats, she still wore her biker gear. "Ready when you are," she said, hunkering down to run a hand over the belly of a greyhound lying on its back in front of her. "And on the drive to the shops I want to hear the complete uncut story of you, a commercial-sized dumpster, and the latest dead body. Right?"

"Who told you?"

"You forget I'm a policewoman and therefore have a special hook-up line with our mutual friend, Detective Inspector Garry Adams. With Scuzz always ready to drop everything the moment you're in trouble, it was a normal thing."

I screwed up my nose at this latest revelation. "Um…might be better if we don't pass that info onto Ben."

She nodded, eyes brimming with laughter. "After almost catching fire from the sparks thrown out by those two earlier today, you could be right."

By the time we found an empty spot in the Supermarket carpark, I'd filled Thunder in on all the gory details–including the mystery of how and why my friend Jules was framed for Mary's murder. Thunder took in the facts, asked a couple of cop-like questions and I could see her brain working overtime to puzzle over my answers.

The supermarket was crowded. Evidently heaps of busy people, just like me, put off food shopping until their refrigerator and cupboards were almost bare. However, today, it looked like we'd all gathered at the shopping center at the same time. "Might be quicker if you go your way and I go mine," I told Thunder as I dragged a trolley from the stack near the entrance. "What say I meet you back at checkout no. 6 in half an hour?"

Nodding agreement, Thunder took off down the chips and chocolate aisle while I squinted at the items on Gran's list. No pre-cooked meals. No chocolate. No ice-cream. No potato chips–just food. Real food. Steak, chops, sausages, chicken, brussel sprouts, potatoes, pumpkin, milk, custard powder, cinnamon, self-raising flour… and on and on it went. What was Gran opening here? A restaurant?

Still grumbling under my breath, I trundled the trolley down the first aisle. Food-shopping was the first thing I'd pass over to Ben's care once we were married. Hey, he ate more than me–let him go buy the stuff. And maybe he could even be the cook every second day. Only fair. One eye on the shopping list and the other on the merchandise, I grabbed food from the shelves, willy-nilly, and tossed it into the trolley. Things like brand and price were irrelevant. Main objective–buy everything on the list and get the heck out of here.

I let out a sigh. It seemed like every minute of my day was double-booked from now until the sun rose on Saturday morning.

Like when Ma rung this morning, her knickers in a double-twist and her patience in a murky ditch. Something about the hire firm being reluctant to set their chairs up on the beach any closer than one hundred meters from the water's edge–which would put my wedding ceremony smack bang in the middle of the seaweed. She'd also booked me in to inspect and taste the wedding cake at 7.00 o-clock tonight which meant Ben would have to take the dogs to the track, while I made nice with the caterers. On top of that, Tanya insisted I pop into her shop before my Hen's party–something about choosing goodies from The Luv Bug to be wrapped and presented to all the 'hens'.

It was while I was simultaneously pondering the cost of fifty gift-wrapped Luv Bug goodies and reaching for a giant-sized bottle of tomato sauce, that disaster struck. A lethal shopping-cart, travelling at least 20 miles over the speed limit, crashed into mine and sent the sauce flying. Unbalanced and hopping on one leg, I watched the bottle cascade high in the air, perform a perfectly executed triple somersault and then plummet missile-like in the direction of ground zero.

"Noooo!" I threw myself at the bottle, missed, and swore as it slammed into the concrete floor with a crash that reverberated throughout the store.

I closed my eyes. Oh God. Not now! I really really had no time for this. Squinting through one half-opened eye, I watched thick red globs of sauce explode from the broken bottle, dance in the air and finally land on the woman who'd been in charge of the speeding cart.

"What the…?" she yelled as she fisted tomato sauce from both eyes and glared at me. "Why don't you look where you're going?" And then recognition made her eyes narrow. "Katrina McKinley? I should have known."

"Patti Murdoch?" Patti was a rival trainer with a handy team of racing dogs. We were usually friendly rivals so I couldn't work out the vehemence in her voice. "You okay?"

"No, thanks to you."

"Me? Patti, you crashed your trolley into mine."

"No I didn't," she shouted as she scrubbed at her clothes with both hands, causing the sauce on the front of her pretty pink top to smear and run down onto the front of her jeans.

I shook my head. Now she looked ten times worse.

"Oh, God, this is just not my day," she said looking down at her jeans. "Nothing's going right." And with a giant hiccup and a face-crumbling sniff, Pattie morphed from a snarling tiger into a teary mess. Snotty tears that when she wiped at her nose with the back of her hand transferred from nose to cheek in streaks.

Anxious to help, I dug around in my pockets but all I could find were three screwed up, fully-used tissues. I jammed them back in my pocket and ordering Patti to stay put, sprinted into the adjoining aisle where I snaffled a box of tissues from the Chemist section of the store.

"Here, use these," I whispered and with a furtive glance over my shoulder, I ripped open the box and passed her two large handfuls of tissues before dropping the packet into my trolley. "Okay, now, is there anything I can do to help?"

By this time, one of the cleaners had arrived with a bucket of water, a dustpan, a mop and a distinctly grumpy face. I mumbled an apology to the cleaner as Thunder rounded the corner and came jogging down the aisle, her trolley veering from side to side on uneven wheels. She pulled up a couple of meters away from us and stood, silently taking in the splatters of sauce that looked like blood, the tears of the mad woman wielding a trolley like a battering ram, and my utter confusion.

"Why don't we leave our shopping carts here and go for a coffee?" she said at last. "If they've been emptied by the time we come back, we'll just start over again." She peered at both Patti and me and frowned. "Looks to me as though you could both do with a caffeine break."

"Good idea." I put my arm around Patti's shoulders and led her to the entrance, half expecting her to snap my arm in two and beat me over the head with both sections. Instead, she trotted along beside me, still sniffing and wiping her nose while Thunder, the practical member of our trio, slipped a twenty-dollar bill to the cleaner and followed us to the coffee-shop next door.

While Thunder ordered coffee and cake for three, I snaffled a table in the corner of the shop and sat Patti on a chair with her back to the door. Her face wasn't a pretty sight. If there'd been a bathroom nearby I'd have taken her there first. "Okay, Patti," I said once she'd settled, wiped her nose again and looked up at me with swollen eyes. "What's going on?"

"Everything…" Patti's bottom lip trembled and before the tears could start up again, I yanked a chair closer and sat beside her. This was unlike Patti. She was normally so motivated, so upbeat. Even when her dog finished last in a race, she'd be the one to smile, congratulate the winner and say something like, 'my dog gave his best–can't ask for more'.

I stared at her, confused. "I've never seen you like this before." And then it hit me. Maybe she'd had bad news from the doctor. I went cold inside. "You're not sick, are you?"

"I'm fine." She sniffed again. "But everything's happening to me at once and I-I can't cope."

"Such as?"

"For a start, my best racer, Collective, broke a hock yesterday."

"Oh, Patti, I'm so sorry. Is he–?"

"No, no. We're getting it operated on and he's going home to his owner to become a couch-potato once he's back on his feet."

"That's good. He's been such a champ on the track, but I know he'll love life on the couch even more."

"I know, but I'll miss him." She gave another sniff. "And the roof sprung a leak during the last rain…"

"That can be fixed."

"And the police came around this morning asking me questions about Mary Parker."

Bingo…now we'd come to the real problem. But why would that make Patti lose her cool? Surely the police had interviewed most greyhound trainers, even with Jules in custody. "Don't worry," I said, putting my hand over hers and squeezing. "They're interviewing everyone. Me included. You're a colleague of Mary's, that's all. What did they want to know?"

Her eyes were red rimmed and swollen as she looked across the table at me. "The police knew about the stand-up fight I had with Mary a few days ago. And-and that I threatened her."

As Thunder placed a tray with three coffees onto the table and slid into the chair next to mine, I studied Patti more closely. Her hair, normally a perfect mane of long straight golden hair that fell artfully around her shoulders like a Princess, was now tangled, messy, as though she'd not long climbed out of bed and hadn't bothered to use a brush. And the puffiness around her eyes had been etched there way before the present crying jag started. "You threatened her?"

Patti looked down at the cup of coffee in front of her for so long I thought she was counting the beans. "Yeah," she said finally. "That bitch had marathon sex with one of my owners in exchange for taking over the training of six of my top race dogs. The slimy creep of an owner only told me he was changing trainers the morning he rocked up to take his dogs from my kennels–only he didn't mention the sex-for-favors that prompted the change. It was Mary who explained that to me in minute detail at the track the same night." A frown furrowed the skin between her eyes as she looked up, eyes narrowed. "And I told her she was a cold-blooded monster that needed to be put down and there was nowhere she could hide from me. I even added that I'd smile while doing everyone a favor."

The cup heading toward my mouth stopped as I gaped at her. Blimey. That made the argument I'd had with Mary look like a kindergarten fall-out. I blinked. "And did anyone hear your threat?"

"Ha!" Patti's laugh sounded more like a dying frog's last croak. "Did anyone hear me? Let's see...only every trainer in the kennel house at the time, the stewards, the track vet, and even the course photographer who'd popped in to ask one of the stewards a question." She pulled at the front of her top. I couldn't stop myself. The whole time I was getting my dog ready for the next race, Mary followed me around, giggling like a school girl, while filling me in on every detail of her sexual campaign and gloating at the new acquisitions to her training-team." Pattie clenched her teeth together so hard I was surprised they didn't splinter. "I swear, Kat, if my hands had been free instead of clasped around a lead while putting on my dog's racing rug, I'd have knocked Mary Parker on her skinny ass."

"And now she's dead," I reminded her.

She clutched the coffee in both hands so fiercely I expected to hear the cup crack. "Yes, Mary's dead," she growled. "But I didn't kill her. Julia Cassidy got to her first."

Patti never struck me as a violent person, in fact just the opposite, but as I watched the way she throttled her cup and heard the ice in her voice as she spoke, I did a hasty rethink.

Maybe Patti reacted so strongly to Mary's treachery that when an opportunity to steal Jules' gun presented itself, she did so, plotting to use the gun to stop Mary from ever hurting another human being.

11

AN HOUR, TWO COFFEES, AND A SECOND GO AT at ticking-off-every-item-on-the-shopping-list later, Thunder and I set off back to the car, our trolleys overflowing with groceries. While stacking bags into the rear of the car, I soon discovered how much Thunder's strength came in handy. For every loaded bag I struggled to lift, she managed four. However, not only was Scuzz's half-sister strong, she was good company. She was intelligent. She could outstare any smart-mouthed adolescent itching to show their newfound hormones with a mere straightening of her shoulders. And she sympathized with how much Patti's latest news affected me.

My mind still in a whirl, I jammed the key into the ignition and started the car. "You know, I'm losing the battle here," I said as I braked to allow a young mother herd three kids all under four across in front of me. "How the heck am I going to prove Jules' innocence? Every time I turn around I stumble over more suspects." I shook my head at Thunder. "I wonder exactly how many female trainers lost their best racing dogs due to Mary sexual conquests?"

"And what does it say about the guys who allowed this to happen?"

"It says they should have their owner's license revoked and their smarmy faces displayed on Facebook for everyone to see."

Thunder gave a deep-throated chuckle. "Or what about pasting their faces on dart boards at all the tracks?"

I sighed. I was fast losing sympathy for the dead woman's unhappy family history. Maybe Mary would have turned out a much nicer person if her little girl had lived–and maybe not. But now, with so much of her dirty-linen to wade through, how was I supposed to unearth the real murderer and get my bridesmaid out of jail and on the beach at Semaphore by sunrise on Saturday?

"You know, even though she upset so many women, it's still more likely a man killed Mary," I told Thunder who had opened a packet of M&M's to share with me on the drive.

"And that's because…"

"Think about it. A female couldn't lift Mary's dead body and toss it into a dumpster."

"I could." Thunder picked out six red M&M's, popped them in her mouth, and shrugged one leather-clad shoulder. "And by the sounds of it–so could your friend, Jules."

I let out a frustrated sigh. "Yeah. 'Spose you're right." Jules, although not a big woman, kept herself in top physical condition. She lifted weights, sparred in the boxing ring, went to the gym, climbed mountains and yes…she could have hurled Mary's body into a dumpster and then continued on jogging.

"Plus, there's usually a way around actions that appear impossible to the uninitiated. In the years I've been in the Force, I've come across some rather inspired crooks. Almost magicians some of them. Let's see," she said and frowned, "if the killer was a woman, she could have stood on a crate and pushed the body bit by bit up and over the top of the dumpster. She could have operated a fork-lift or used a ladder. Or our murderer might have been two people–one to shoot the victim, while the other one helped dispose of the body."

"Hmm…never thought of that." My fingers tightened on the wheel. Bad enough worrying about one murderer. I didn't like the idea of looking for two.

"Still, as you say, the killer is more likely to have been male," Thunder continued, looking as though she could go all day thinking up murder methods. "After all, from what you've told me, there were plenty of pissed off guys on Mary Parker's ravished-and-dumped list. Like that guy, Peter, you mentioned earlier. Now he had a motive, in spades. The poor misguided individual lost his house, his wife, and his kids because Mary lured him into her bed, made sure his wife found out, and then tossed him to the curb." She shook her head. "What a class-one bitch."

"And that's putting it mildly."

"Anyway, maybe he confronted her, she laughed at him once too often and he killed her."

"I'd agree, but I can't see Peter using Jules' gun to frame her. Peter really likes Jules. She allows him use her straight track and whenever he wants to bath his dogs he lets himself into her treatment room and uses the hydro bath."

"Having carte blanche to your friend's property would make it that much easier for him to steal her gun."

"Maybe." But I wasn't convinced. Even though the hearing-deficient, visually-impaired, Centenarian from over the road thought he'd seen Peter's van near her property the morning Jules' guns went missing, something about the way Peter looked at Jules when he thought she wasn't watching, made me think he had more than friendly feelings toward her.

"Anyway, why don't we pay Peter a visit? I'd like to check out the guy's body language when you inform him you have a witness who saw his van outside Jules' property the morning her guns went missing." A grin spread across Thunder's face and she raised one eyebrow. "I don't want to brag, but interpreting body language is one of my specialties. Ask Scuzz, I was dux of my class in that subject at Cop-school."

"Hey, brag away," I told her as we arrived home and I slowed to a halt in front of my much-loved Kat McKinley Greyhound Kennels sign. "Any and all sleuthing skills are gratefully accepted."

"Just remember, you're not on your own for this one."

"Didn't think for a minute I would be." I grinned at her through the car window as she opened the gate and collected several letters from my letter box. "So…how about we drop in and check Peter's body language tonight?" My grin widened to show her exactly how keen I was to get my friend Jules out of a jail cell and into her teal blue bridesmaid's dress. "I know for a fact he has no dogs racing, but I can always give him a ring and see if he's home."

"No, let's surprise him. If he's not there we can always have a bit of a snoop around and catch up with him first thing tomorrow morning."

"Sounds good to me."

"What time suits?"

"Let's see, Ben's taking the racing dogs to the track tonight while I attend some wacky, out-of-the-blue, wedding-cake tasting-ritual that starts at seven o'clock. Why I booked this crazy baker, I don't know, but he said over the phone he was a good friend of my sister, Liz. That should have put me off, but I felt sorry for him. Anyway, I can drive back here afterwards and pick you up, say around 7.30 or a little later. That okay with you?"

As I drove the car through, Thunder closed the gate behind me before sliding back onto the passenger seat. "Excellent timing," she said tossing the pile of letters onto the seat between us and closing the car door. "Big Brother's going out with cousin Jake tonight so we won't have him tagging along behind us." She screwed up her nose. "Don't know how many times I've told him I'm quite capable of taking care of myself. In fact, I've proven it by repeatedly beating the muscle-head in arm wrestling, but do you think he'll listen?"

I gave her an eye roll for an answer. I knew exactly how protective Scuzz could be and although he was great to have around in a scary situation, he could become a tad stifling at times. I looked down at the letters piled between us. Mostly either asking or demanding money. But the envelope on top with no address had me frowning. Could be a note from a disgruntled neighbor. One of Ben's dogs hadn't settled into his new kennel and was inclined to voice his disapproval rather loudly at times. I picked it up and tore open the top of the envelope with my teeth while piloting the car one-handed toward the house. "Just remembered, we have to pop into The Luv Bug on the way to Peter's," I told Thunder. "Tanya wants me to choose gifts for the Hen's party tomorrow night." I sighed at the thought. "Of course I could leave the choice to her but I can't trust my best friend's warped sense of humor."

After parking as close to the front door as I could manage–lots of groceries to haul inside the house–I shook a single sheet of paper from the envelope. And frowned. For a moment, the words staring up at me didn't compute. Cut from a colored magazine and pasted onto the white paper, the message danced in front of my eyes.

BUTT OUT OR YOU'LL BE NEXT TO DIE.

Who? What? And how did the author of these words know I'd been asking questions? Was it someone I knew? My heart pounded and my throat closed over making it difficult to breathe. And the question that had me close to wetting my pants–was it a threat to kill me or was it someone's idea of a sick joke?

"You okay, Kat?" Thunder, hand on the car door ready to climb out, glanced across at me and frowned. "You look like you've seen a ghost."

My heart still flip-flopping on the floor of the car, I passed the sheet of paper over and watched her scowl down at the words. Swearing, she yanked the car door open and swung out onto the gravel. "This is serious shit, Kat." Tight lipped, she pulled a phone from inside her leather jacket. "I'm contacting DI Adams."

"Not much he can do," I said, wishing it was different. "The envelope's blank and the letters are cut out of a magazine."

"Doesn't matter. I'll get Adams to send someone straight over here to pick up the envelope and the note and take them back to the station. Maybe forensics can find something."

The swarm of butterflies fluttering around in the pit of my stomach magnified. "Can't see anyone being careless enough to leave their fingerprints behind, can you?"

"It's worth a try."

I listened to her speaking to DI Adams over the phone and the more anxious her voice became the crazier the butterflies responded. I'd had a death threat like this before, back when Scuzz was my bodyguard. I guess I had to be thankful for one thing. At least this death-threat didn't come with bloody animal body parts attached, like the first time.

"Don't mention this to any of the others. Especially Gran and Fred," I told Thunder as she pocketed her phone, popped the note into a plastic baggie produced from the inside pocket of her black leather jacket and came around to help me unload my groceries. "If they think I'm in danger, Fred might decide to exchange his toy gun for a real one and I'd feel safer with the writer of the note than a half-blind Fred toting a real gun."

Leaving her own groceries in the car, Thunder, muscles bulging, once again hefted four bags to my one into the house and onto the kitchen table.

"Where's Tater?" I asked Gran. Yolo and Lucky were twisting themselves inside out, barking, and diving in and out between my legs in their goofball attempt to show me how happy they were to see me. Then, while Yolo pushed her head up under my hand for a pat, Lucky grabbed her stuffed purple wombat from under the kitchen table and ran around in circles making it squeak. But my fun-loving Chihuahua, usually the first to greet me, wasn't to be seen.

"Take a peek." Gran, already busy packing groceries away, indicated the lounge room with a nod of her head. I poked my nose around the corner and grinned. There was Fred, a newspaper opened on his lap, his glasses half-mast, fast asleep on one of my lounge chairs. Tater, also asleep, was tucked under one arm. The dog's little black eyes opened when he heard me, but evidently quite comfortable where he was, he merely gave a little wriggle, snuggled closer to Fred, and went back to sleep.

Until that moment I'd been worried about leaving my dogs with virtual strangers for a week. Now I could see that wasn't going to be a problem. Unlike Ma, who was allergic to 'those dirty smelly dogs', Gran and Fred actually seemed to love my precious fur-balls. Maybe I could talk them into adopting one of our GAP greyhounds. And I knew which one the perfect choice would be. Petunia. The little white and black greyhound with the soulful eyes. She was such a sweet well-behaved girl she'd make an ideal pet for senior citizens and Fred and Gran could share her with the other residents of the Aged Care facility.

Shelving this brilliant idea until after the honeymoon, I tossed my car keys across the table to Thunder. A feminine version of her half-brother, Thunder's body filled the doorway. Same father but different mothers–it was amazing how alike they were. "Here, drive the car to the granny-flat and unload your lot," I told her. "I'll be there soon."

Gran, busy packing tomatoes, lettuce and cheese into the refrigerator, spoke to me over her shoulder. "There were a few phone calls while you were away, Katrina. Your mother, bless her heart, rang to remind you about the cake tasting at seven …"

"Again?"

She nodded with a roll of her eyes which on my once sour-faced Gran, made me grin. "Also, the airways rang to verify your flight times. A delivery man knocked on the door with several crates of dogs' meat–I sent him down to see Ben or Jake at the kennel-house–and there was a phone call from your wedding celebrant."

'What did Delta have to say?"

"Not a lot, other than it was in the stars that your day would be perfect on Saturday." Gran shook her head. "You know, I wouldn't be surprised if that woman is ten beer bottles short of a crate."

Chuckling, I picked up the empty bags from the floor and stored them for re-use. "Maybe even twelve."

"Oh, yes, and your wedding dress arrived while you were away, so I hung it in your wardrobe." She stopped packing and turned toward me, her smile dreamy, her face alight with an inner glow. "It was lovely to see it again. Did you know, Katrina, I wore that same dress when I married your grandfather, bless his stinking socks, almost sixty years ago."

"No way! I knew Ma wore the dress but…you too?" I wasn't sure whether that was good news or bad. "So, my wedding dress is close to sixty years old?"

"And it's just as beautiful as the day I bought it. You'll look like a princess when you walk down the aisle–at the beach." She let out a choked laugh as she forced a side of beef into an almost full freezer. "Your mother was so peeved that you weren't marrying in a church, the day she rung to tell me about it, I was afraid she'd have a seizure."

"I know, Gran, but Ben and I love the ocean and we feel God can see us just as well at the beach than he can inside a church. In fact, better. He can look down on us from the sky and give us his blessing."

Gran threw both arms around me and drew me in for a hug. "Don't worry about your mother. She'll get over it. And if she doesn't–you can tell her you know all about how she lost her virginity at aged sixteen."

"She what?"

"That's all I'm saying. But of course, she doesn't need to know that. Now, what else happened while you were away?" Gran stared down at the two greyhounds who'd given up showing off and were now sound asleep on the floor, Yolo with her four legs in the air. "Oh yes, I remember what else I had to tell you. Lucky dug a hole in the backyard and buried one of her purple toys. A dinosaur, I think. I figured she was worried Yolo was out to steal it."

I collapsed into a chair and laughed. Whatever games Fred and Gran played in the bedroom together, I totally approved. With bells on. This Gran in my kitchen today was so far removed from the grandmother I knew while I was growing up, she was barely recognizable. Not just chalk and cheese but frog and princess. And then I remembered Grandpa, who I'd never seen smile in all the years I'd known him. Grandpa, whose face was set in a scowl until the day he died and who barked orders at everyone, including Gran. Maybe he'd sapped the spark right out of the young girl he married and Fred, with his kindly eyes and cheeky wit, had found a way to relight the embers.

And I loved Fred for that.

After reading that threatening note, Gran's warm hug and her laughter was the best medicine I could ask for. Came close to melting the icy lump of fear lodged firmly in my chest.

12

The cake tasting ceremony was a fizzle from start to end.

A long-haired hippie guy, complete with scruffy beard, a bad case of acne, a nose ring that had gone a strange greenish color and dressed in a starched white chef's outfit, presented me with the tiniest sliver of wedding cake on a gold-edged plate. With his solemn expression, unseen music in the background playing something highly classical, and the pompous manner in which he offered me the plate–you'd have thought I was being presented with The Elixir of Life.

I downed the morsel in one swallow–told the guy it was yum–and stood up to leave.

The entire ritual would have been all over in three minutes, top, except for Ma, who demanded she have a taste of the cake too. The hippie chef refused on the grounds she was neither the bride nor the groom. But Ma wouldn't back down–after all, she'd paid for the damn cake. Long story short, Ma and the hippie chef spent the next twenty minutes dueling–not with swords but tongues–until Ma won the tournament. Then, reluctantly digging another bite-sized smidgen of cake from somewhere it could easily be covered up later with icing, the chef plonked it down in front of her. No plate. No ceremony.

Still, Ma was appeased and when I dropped her off out the front of her house she was even quite mellow, saying how much she looked forward to my Hen's party the following night. Yeah. Right. Tanya and

I had already arranged to pump her so full of alcohol early on in the evening that she'd be asleep before the real entertainment appeared–an all-man band comprising of six strippers.

So, it was close to 8 o'clock by the time Thunder and I, on our way to see Peter, pulled up out the front of The Luv Bug. I shouldered my way through the glass doors, only to find the shop's manager, Norm, pumping up a sex doll with a foot pump. Thunder did a double-take, her eyebrows meeting over her nose. To make her introduction to The Luv Bug even more bizarre, Norm was wearing long white ballet tights and a floppy pink top while Tanya stacked shelves in an almost-not-there, miniscule fairy costume.

"If you two plan on starring in The Dance of the Sugar Plum Fairy, you need to fill your tights out more," I told Norm, bending down to squeeze one of his calves. "As I thought… I've felt marshmallows harder than your muscles." I tutted with disapproval. "How do you expect to lift the fairy without dropping her?"

"I'll have you know, I'm fitter than I look. I walk to work one morning a week."

I shook my head at him, trying hard not to grin. "Walking's not enough, Norman. Maybe you should become a member of one of those gyms you're always rubbishing. Attend classes. Work out on their equipment. Or, if you don't want to be shown up by the jocks, maybe you could buy yourself a pair of those short-shorts and a tank top and go jogging before breakfast every morning. You'll soon have the ladies hanging out their windows whistling as you run past. What d'you think?"

After Norm had finished telling me exactly what he thought of my suggestions, I introduced him to Thunder, my biker friend–the one whose muscles made Norm look like the skinny kid on the beach getting sand kicked in his face. They seemed to strike it off, so I left them discussing the pros and cons of selling pink fluffy handcuffs as opposed to the real deal, while I joined Tanya.

My best friend was holding up two of the weird metal type thingies she'd been unpacking. "Hey, Kat, why not buy your Hens a set of these for tomorrow night's gift?"

I took the two metal type thingies from and studied them more closely. Hmm. Looked like stationery you'd use in an office. "What are they?"

"Nipple clamps."

"Ugh!" I dropped them like they were red hot.

"Or what about butt plugs?" said the sex-addled fairy whose wings were starting to droop and fray at the edges.

I shook my head at her. "You know where you can put those!"

Tanya's eyes sparkled. "Yeah, I do actually—but don't ask for a demonstration."

"Demonstration of what?" asked Norm as he closed off the valve on his blow-up doll—a creature of unnatural proportions—and straightened up.

"Don't ask!" Tanya and I said in unison.

"An interesting shop you have here," said Thunder picking up an item that could have been used to unblock a sink but I wasn't game to ask how customers of an Adult shop would actually use it.

"No," I butted in before either Tanya or Norm could debunk the mystery of the big rubber sucker, "I'll have fifty fancy garter belts. That'll do for the Hens."

"Are you sure?" said Tanya frowning as though I'd lost the plot. "Not very imaginative."

"I'd rather be called unimaginative than have to call an ambulance for Ma after she tore off the gift wrapping and discovered nipple clamps and a butt plug."

"Okay, okay. But I insist you include a packet of these little beauties with each garter belt. Just to brighten up the night. After all, it's a Hens' party–not a Mothers' meeting." She trotted across to the other side of the shop and returned with a large cardboard box. "These little babies are the latest to come in. Fruit flavored rippled condoms. There are six in a pack, and each condom smells and tastes like a different fruit." She held a sample up for us to see and began reading from the side of the packet. "Let's see, in each pack we have a banana, an orange, an apple, a strawberry, a lime and a blackberry flavored condom, all with specially molded ripples that are guaranteed to create sexual friction to a woman's G spot." She looked up and must have noticed the look of horror on Thunder's face. After years of hearing Tanya spout her wares, I was immune to any of her sex-rated sales pitches but my new leather-clad friend wasn't. Her face was the same color as the strawberry flavored condom.

"Tan, can you just get your foot out of your mouth for half a minute and box my stuff up? We're going to interrogate Peter Findlay. Thunder says she wants to check out his body language–see if he's lying."

"Ooh, ooh, you can't go without me." Tanya, saggy wings flapping, danced up and down on the spot. "'Cos while Thunder studies Peter's body language, I can listen to what he's saying between the lines."

"But–"

"Come on, Kat, you know you need my know-how. You might be good at picking up clues, but you're way too gullible.'

"Am not!"

"Am too. You're hopeless. You're always so busy looking for the good in people they pull the wool over your eyes and then run off with your best china."

"So what? My best china only cost me $6.50 at Target." Okay, that sounded like a petulant teenager, but Tanya was getting too close to the truth.

With a one-shouldered shrug, Tanya began packing garter belts and condom packets into an empty cardboard box which had previously housed battery-operated whips–it said so on the label–and then turned to her boss. "I'm off now, Norm. You've already had me working ten hours overtime this week. That's enough," she said before turning back to me. "It's okay, Erin's staying with her no-good lazy father tonight so give me five minutes to finish up here, grab my overcoat and I'll follow you to Peter's house in my car. Okay?"

I grinned. How could it not be okay? Thunder might be an excellent friend to have around if the situation turned nasty, but Tania was my sleuthing buddy. She'd been with me every time I came in contact with a dead body. She'd forced me to pull up my big girl pants whenever things got tough. And she was my best friend.

It was close to 8.30 when we pulled up outside Peter's suburban house in Elizabeth, a rental property that was badly in need of repair. His ex-wife claimed the house they'd bought during their marriage in the divorce settlement and promptly sold it and moved interstate with another guy, taking the children with her. Now, all thanks to Mary Parker and his own weakness, Peter had no family, no house, no job due to being put off, and only the dogs to keep him from giving up.

Although the house was in complete darkness, Peter's green van was parked in the driveway, which meant he was at home. I could see a light on around the back, indicating he was probably in the dog shed treating the race dogs. Most likely one of the dogs that raced yesterday was up on the table and Peter was either checking for injuries or machining their sore muscles with the laser or ultrasonic. The guy might not look after himself– but no one could ever accuse him of not looking after his dogs.

As Thunder and I made our way down the side of the house, Tanya, the buttons on her heavy overcoat undone revealing her ballet tutu and squashed wings, joined us. "Geez," she said, grabbing my arm for support as she lost her footing and staggered into a hole. "The ruts in this driveway are so deep Peter could fill them up with water and charge trainers to come and swim their greyhounds."

It was a hazardous trip from the front to the back of Peter' house but after negotiating a dog trailer, several rubbish bins, and stepping over a discarded bike, we finally arrived at the dog shed in one piece. I banged on the door. "Peter? You in there?"

All we could hear was a loud cacophony of barking followed by one dog squealing, so I pushed the door open and walked in. My two assistants, Body Language Expert and Reading Between the Lines Expert, hot on my heels.

There was no Peter, but his four dogs were leaping around in their kennels, almost turning themselves inside-out to show their pleasure at seeing us. One dog's water dish had been tipped over, another had ripped up her bedding and their barking sounded stressed. Okay, it was normal for dogs to be happy to have company, but these dogs were frantic. And then I saw why. On the bench beside the sink were four dog bowls, all made up for tea. 8.30 at night and Peter hadn't fed his dogs?

Something was drastically wrong.

I walked to the little office he'd blocked off at the end of the shed and pushed the door open. The desk, as usual, was covered in unpaid bills, greyhound magazines, dirty coffee cups, broken leads waiting to be fixed and a battered laptop. But no Peter. I shook my head and went to walk away, when a familiar note caught my eye. A note with the words, 'BUTT OUT OR YOU'LL BE NEXT TO DIE'. The words cut from magazines and pasted onto a blank sheet–exactly the same as mine.

An icy lump formed in my chest and my throat felt drier than an empty water bottle. Was Peter the initiator of these notes? Was he cutting out letters and gluing them onto paper and then sending them to anyone questioning Mary's murder–or, like me, did he discover the threatening message in his letterbox? And if so, why would he be investigating Mary's murder when he hated her so much?

Because he loved Jules and wanted her out of prison.

I snatched the note off the desk and stared at the cut-out letters. And then, feeling as though I was going to throw up, screwed the paper into a ball and shoved it deep into my back pocket. As soon as I found Peter, I'd confront him. Find out if he was the person behind the threats or, like me, a victim.

As I left the office and stumbled into the kennel area, I decided not to show the note to Thunder and Tanya yet. I wasn't ready to talk about the implications of finding an identical threat to mine hiding amongst the unpaid bills and out-of-date race-books on Peter's desk. My heart was crashing around in my chest so much I'd probably have a heart attack if either Thunder or Tanya freaked out about it. I was freaking out enough for the three of us.

"Something's drastically wrong here," said Tanya as she rescued the empty water dish from the first kennel and carried it across to the sink for a refill. "It's like Peter was standing here preparing the dogs' teas and suddenly got zapped up by aliens."

I let out a shaky breath. "How about you two feed the dogs while I check inside the house and see if he's in there. There's no light on, but he could have felt dizzy, gone inside to lie down, and before he could switch on the light, fainted."

"Unlikely," said Thunder studying the four bowls on the bench as though debating whether it was legal to feed someone else's dogs without their knowledge.

"But the only plausible reason." Tanya, with no such qualms, grabbed two dog bowls and headed toward the stressed-out canines who'd been left staring at their food for God knows how long, with no way of reaching it. "I mean, even if Peter was called away on an emergency, he'd feed the dogs before he left."

Tanya was right. So, with thoughts of that note spinning around in my head, I stumbled across the uneven lawn toward the house, almost twisting my right ankle in a deep pothole and opened the back door.

"Peter! Are you in there?"

No answer. Geez it was dark. Two steps inside and I bumped into what felt like a washing machine. And only by stretching my hands out in front of me saved me from slamming face-first into the kitchen door. Once through the second door and in what I knew to be the kitchen, I felt along the wall for the switch, found it and turned on the light.

It was like a bomb had hit the room. Chairs overturned. Broken crockery lay scattered on the floor. A pot of what looked like stew had been upended, splattering the walls, the stove and spewing down onto the green and gray lino underneath.

And in the middle of the chaos, his dull unwashed hair caked in blood, his face sheet-white, eyes staring at nothing, mouth open in what appeared to be a soundless scream, lay Peter Findlay.

"Omygod! Please, please, Peter, please be okay." Jerking my mobile out of my jeans' pocket to ring for an ambulance, I rushed across the room and threw myself onto the floor beside him, one knee sliding in blood. "Peter, can you hear me?" I dropped my phone and rolled him from his side onto his back, then took a hold of both shoulders and shook him. "Wake up, Peter. Please, wake up."

With each shake, Peter's head flopped against the blood-stained floor like a limp noodle. Thump. Thump. Thump. "Come on, wake up!" I shouted, my voice becoming more and more hysterical. "You have to tell me who did this to you."

It was obvious someone had caved Peter's head in. But who? Was it the anonymous note writer? Was I going to end up like this too? I reached out and touched Peter's head and my hand came away sticky with blood. This wasn't happening. Not again. Maybe I could bring him around by giving him CPR. "Thunder!" I screamed at the top of my voice. "Tanya, come in here!"

Tanya and Thunder exploded through the kitchen doorway, both calling out to me. But while Tanya stopped on the threshold, her face losing its color as she took in the overturned chairs, the chaos in the room, and Peter lying in a pool of blood on the floor, Thunder morphed into policewoman mode.

"Is this Peter Findlay?"

I nodded. Yes, this was the poor guy who'd already lost everything dear to him in life.

"Have you moved him?"

"Rolled him on his back."

"Have you touched anything?"

"Only Peter."

"When you came in, was the room like this?"

I blinked. "Yes." Surely she didn't think I'd gone berserk and trashed the room.

"And have you rung the police?"

"Not yet." I indicated my mobile on the floor with a nod of my head then, still on my knees, leant forward, feeling for a pulse on the side of Peter's neck. Not a flicker. No, no, maybe that wasn't the right spot. I could hear Thunder explaining about Peter's predicament on the phone close to my ear. Seemed like she'd given up on him already. Ignoring her, I tried again, this time wrapping my fingers around his left wrist. Come on. Come on. Beat, damn you. Beat.

After feeling both wrists and the side of the neck again, I dropped my hand to my side and closed my eyes. I felt my best friend, Tanya, kneel down beside me and sniffed back a sob as she wrapped one arm around my shoulders in a hug. "Is he–?"

Unable to speak through the lump in my throat, I nodded. Peter had a perfectly good reason for not returning to feed his dogs. He couldn't–he was dead.

13

Thunder, her mobile plastered to her ear, was discussing 'the deceased' and 'the body' with whoever was on the other end, as though poor Peter was a lump of raw meat instead of a fellow human being. Okay, she was a policewoman and trained to hide her feelings plus she didn't actually know Peter, but hey, he was right there on the floor beside her, his head smashed to pulp, no heartbeat, and his loyal dogs now without their beloved master.

I could hear Tanya's breath becoming raspier as she squatted beside me, her body tense, like a cork ready to pop. I squeezed her hand and when she looked up, flicked her a look of understanding. This wasn't good. She blinked back at me, mumbling something that sounded like, Holy freakin' crapshoot! I agreed. How many times had we been through this before? You'd think, after seeing your first dead body, subsequent corpses would be easier to stomach–but believe me, that wasn't how it worked. Tanya returned my squeeze and scrambled to her feet, her face taking on a greenish tinge. Then, legs suddenly uncooperative, she stumbled across to Peter's refrigerator. And not taking time to examine the childish crayon drawings pinned to the front with fridge magnets, she yanked the door open and stuck her head inside.

"Tanya, you can't do that!" Thunder, almost dropping her cell phone, let out a yelp. "Can't you see this is a crime scene?"

Tanya turned her back and dragged two cans from the fridge. "I think the dead body on the floor is a big enough giveaway, don't you?" She tossed a can to me and shook her head as she studied the inside of the fridge again. "Holy freakin' crapshoot! That's it. There's no more beer in here." She slammed the fridge door shut and appeared to dance on the spot. "Wonder if there's any more stashed in one of the other rooms?"

"But you can't–"

"May as well save your breath," I told Thunder, righting a chair so I could sit down before my legs collapsed under me. I ripped the tab off the can and took a swig. "Trust me. If Tan doesn't find any more booze she'll start swinging from the lightbulbs and screaming like a cat with its tail jammed in a car door. When she's subjected to the sight and smell of a dead body the only remedy is for her to get legless drunk."

Thunder frowned. I expected her to freak out completely, but she surprised me. I guess she wasn't my adored friend, Scuzz's half-sister for nothing. "Okay," she said her voice gentle as she disconnected her phone and peered down at Peter. "I'm afraid we can't do any more for this poor guy. Whoever hit him over the head did a damn good job of it. So, here's what we're gonna do. We'll get our butts out of the crime scene so the police can do their job when they arrive and we'll wait for them in the dog shed."

Tanya shook her head. "But I need more–"

"It's okay. When I checked the fridge in the dog shed earlier, I noticed two six packs in amongst the dogs' meat." She grinned at Tanya who'd finished her can of beer and was wiping at a frothy moustache with the back of her hand. "You know, I could do with a shot of nerve tonic myself."

Sipping at my can of beer, I slowly looked around the room, taking in the chaos left by the intruder. Was this caused by them fighting, or was it intentional? And did the intruder leave the murder weapon behind or take it with him? I ducked my head under the kitchen table, but all I could see were dishes and broken plates. And to kill a guy as big as Peter they'd need to hit him with something a lot more solid than a Cheap as Chips soup bowl.

I finished my drink, stood up, and squashing my empty beer can tossed it in the kitchen bin. "What say we have a quick snoop around for clues before we leave?"

"No!" Thunder jumped up and fished the can out of the bin, transferring it to her pocket. "You'd be disturbing the crime scene. Now, come on, let's leave everything as is and get the hell out of here." She rolled her eyes. "Thank God you two don't accompany me when I'm working."

I took one last look at Peter. When I'd touched him, his skin was cold. And judging by the fact the dogs had missed out on their evening meal, I guessed he must have been dead for around three hours. It didn't seem real. We'd been talking to Peter at the Port wharf only that morning and now he was dead.

"Wonder if this is the murder weapon?" said Tanya pulling me out of my thoughts and indicating a heavy doorstop in the shape of a greyhound, half-hidden by the refrigerator. She squatted down beside it. "Yep. The greyhound's head is covered in blood."

"Don't touch it!" Thunder raced across and grabbed Tanya's arm. "This is a classic case of a burglary gone wrong. With any luck the thief wasn't wearing gloves because he didn't think he'd be disturbed. He could have left finger-prints on the murder weapon."

"S'pose so," said Tanya but didn't sound convinced. It was like she was metaphorically rolling her eyes at the thought of a burglar so dumb he'd tootle off to commit a robbery and leave his gloves at home in his dresser drawer.

As I followed Thunder and Tanya across the neglected lawn and into the dog shed, alarm bells kept going off in my head. A burglary gone wrong? Maybe Thunder was right. Maybe Peter heard a noise, discovered he was being robbed, fought with the intruder and been bashed over the head with the doorstopper. Maybe. Or could Peter's death be all to do with the threatening note currently burning a hole in my pocket?

Fifteen minutes later, after settling Peter's dogs down for the night, I sat huddled in the back seat of a police car. We'd been separated for questioning as soon as the police arrived on the scene. The fact that Thunder produced her police warrant and Tanya, her coat discarded, danced around in her fairy costume singing I'm a Little Teapot on top note–she'd downed ten beers in fifteen minutes–made not a scrap of difference to the officers.

I looked through the car window as headlights and spotlights blazed across Peter's house, turning night into day. I watched uniformed cops scurry like ants across the lawn and down Peter's driveway where DI Adams' black monster of a car was parked. Saw the DI shuffle through the front doorway after viewing the body and wander across to the police car in front of mine to take Tanya's statement. Good luck there. Tanya would be either fast asleep, still singing or she'd be trying to sell him the latest in sex toys.

But all I really wanted was for Ben to come screaming down the road in his van, brake to a stop and insist on taking me home. I sighed and wrapped my arms around my body to keep warm. While watching Tanya get legless drunk in the dog shed, I'd tried to get through to my fiancé but his phone kept going to voice mail, so I'd left a text explaining what had happened in the hope he'd pick up his phone and check for messages. I needed Ben's arms wrapped around me, melting the chill in my bloodstream. Ben's lips warming my face, my neck, my body. His deep throated chuckle cracking the icicles around my heart. I didn't want to be sitting in the back of a police car, shivering, with unanswerable questions repeating themselves over and over in my brain. Questions like: Who would want to kill Peter? Was it a thief who broke into the house while Peter was out the back and then decided to bash him over the head with a blunt instrument when he was caught in the act? Or did Peter's death have everything to do Mary Parker's murder?

I closed my eyes. Of course it did. I'd seen the note. The note identical to mine. Peter must have been asking questions, wanting to help his friend, Jules, and he'd paid the ultimate penalty for snooping.

Would I be next?

At last the door of the car in front of me opened and DI Adams scrambled out, still talking. His hair looked even more in need of a brush than usual and his suit coat hung off his shoulders. He strode toward me, dragged the car door open and eased his body inside. "Any idea why she's dressed up as a fairy?" he asked as he shook his head and slumped back in the seat beside me.

"Tanya came straight from work."

"Should have guessed." He looked at me more closely. "You okay?"

I nodded.

He raised one skeptical eyebrow at me before slowly entwining his fingers together on his lap. "So, here you are again–in the wrong place at the wrong time?"

"Seems like it."

"Any particular reason?"

I shrugged trying to act all nonchalant. "We just called in to say hello. Since his divorce, Peter's been fighting depression. We were passing by, so thought we'd call in and cheer him up. You know, good deed for the day–that sort of thing."

"At this time of night? Less than two days before your wedding?" He lifted one eyebrow and shook his head. "Don't think so." He brushed what looked like biscuit crumbs from the front of his baggy suit and settled more deeply into the seat. "Take your time, Katrina. I've got all night."

I looked down at my lap, let out a deep sigh. No way did I want to spend all night in the back seat of a police car with DI Adams for company. "Okay, okay, we called in to see Peter because I wanted to ask him some questions about Mary Parker's death. Happy now?"

"No, I'm not happy now. Far from it. Mary Parker's murder has nothing to do with you, so–"

"What do you mean? I found her body therefore it has everything to do with me."

"That's where you're wrong. You might have found Mary's body, and although that must have been very traumatic for you, now it's up to us, the police, to track down her murderer and bring him or her to justice–not you."

"But–"

"And by coming here tonight–intent on sticking your nose where there was every likelihood it would be cut off and fed to the dogs–you've stumbled over another body and been found in the middle of another crime scene."

"Yes, but–"

"I. Haven't. Finished. Yet." He growled each word separately and I swear smoke was coming out of his ears. "And did you ever stop to think, what if you'd gone looking for Peter inside the house while the thief was still in there? What if you'd caught him not only stealing Peter's valuables but with a murder weapon in his hand and a dead body at his feet? What do you think he'd do, Katrina? Shake your hand? Make you a cup of tea with milk and two sugars? No, he'd use the murder weapon on you too–just on the off-chance you might recognize him in a line-up."

Okay, I refused to follow that theory to its obvious conclusion on the grounds it would give me nightmares. Instead, I sniffed. "Poor Peter. From the moment he came in contact with Mary Parker, the stars have been aligned against him."

"Don't know about the stars but whoever he interrupted in his kitchen tonight was definitely against him. As was the doorstopper that proved harder than Peter's head."

I cleared my throat. If DI Adam's strategy was to scare the socks off me, I'd give him an A+ grading. In my mind, I could still see Peter's dead staring eyes, the open wound turning his head into meat. I closed my eyes. Maybe it was time to come clean. Inhaling a shaky breath, I mumbled, "What if it wasn't a burglar who killed Peter?"

His eyes narrowed into slits. "Is there something you haven't told me?"

As my hand crept into the pocket of my jacket and wrapped itself around the screwed up note inside, I nodded, not wanting to be right.

"I had a gut feeling you knew more about this than you're letting on." A frown wrinkled the DI's forehead and his eyes narrowed even further. "Spit it out! If a burglar didn't bash Peter Findlay's head in, who did?"

"The same person who murdered Mary Parker."

"Whaat?" He looked down his nose at me as though I'd lost the plot. "Peter's death had nothing to do with Mary Parker's murder. This was a break in."

I dragged the note from my pocket, flattened it out and passed it across to him. "I found this on the desk in Peter's office."

DI Adams' mouth opened and shut several times but no words came out. He took the note, read it and closed his eyes on something between a snarl and a sigh.

"It's not my fault.' I jumped in before he could open his mouth and scream at me. Before he could rip strips off my skin and leave me in handcuffs with a ten-year jail sentence hanging over my head for obstructing the course of justice, or whatever else he could dream up. "Peter wasn't dead when I took this…well, he was, but I didn't know he was dead…and…and I was going to have it out with him. Confront him. I figured Peter was either the one clipping letters out of magazines and sending the notes, or, like me, he'd had the death threat delivered to his letterbox."

DI Adams opened his eyes, looked at me, but still didn't speak. He seemed to be counting to twenty-five in his head.

I fidgeted with the buckle on the seat belt beside me. "So, you see, finding this note in Peter's office sorta complicates things. His murderer mightn't have been a burglar after all. It might have been someone waiting for him to come inside, the doorstopper already in his or her hand ready to strike. Then, after killing Peter, he–or she–messed up the kitchen to make it look like a burglary."

He sighed, seemed to sink further into the upholstery and finally spoke, his words so soft I had to lean closer to hear him. "You've done it again, Katrina. You've removed evidence from a crime scene."

"But it wasn't a crime scene when I took it," I wailed, waving my arms in the air to emphasize the fact. "It was just Peter's untidy office. And when I saw this note, exactly like mine, in amongst all the rubbish he piles on his desk, I had to take it. And-and if he hadn't been lying dead in his kitchen, I'd-I'd have …" I let out a loud sniff and dug into the pocket of my jeans for a tissue. Why did I always find myself slap bang in the middle of trouble? "It was awful," I croaked, trying to push words through my blistered throat. "There were bits of Peter's brains splattered in amongst the blood. And-and this dirty great hole in his head. And-and his eyes…oh, God, his eyes…"

There was a thunderous knock on the car window beside me. I jumped, my heart flipping and flopping like a fish on a jetty. Swallowing, struggling to get some saliva to moisten my dry throat, I looked up and let out a hysterical laugh.

It was Ben. My Ben. The gorgeous man I'd be exchanging life-time vows with in less than thirty hours' time. He'd plastered his face against the window of the locked car, nose flattened, mouth open, eyes peering into the interior. Evidently checking to make sure he had the right car and it was me incarcerated inside. When I waved to him, he stepped back and banged on the window with his fist.

"Open up!" he yelled. "I'm here to take my fiancé home."

14

From the passenger seat of Ben's van, I watched the DI and Ben pace up and down on the footpath in front of Peter's house. Listened to their raised voices. Cringed at their animated body language. And I knew they were talking about me. My throat closed over as I slumped further down in my seat trying to make myself smaller. And when Peter's shrouded body was carried through the front door on a stretcher and loaded into an ambulance with no siren and no lights, it almost seemed surreal. Like I was on a movie set and any minute someone would say CUT and Peter would hop up off the stretcher and go have a cup of tea while waiting for the next take. Shaking myself, I grabbed a dog blanket from behind the seat, embracing the familiar smell of dogs and Cheezels, Ben's favorite snack, and wrapped its comforting warmth around me.

I should never have got involved in Mary's murder in the first place. What was I thinking? It wasn't as though I was a professional PI and being paid big bucks to ask questions or look for clues. And it wasn't as though I had lots of time on my hands. Geez, I was getting married on Saturday, plus there was all the planning involved in making sure said wedding magically happened. That's all I should be thinking about. Okay, my friend, Jules, was in custody–but she was innocent. She didn't need my bumbling help to prove it. All I'd done so far was make the situation worse. And now Peter was dead.

And whoever killed Peter and Mary was most likely, at this very moment, busy planning their next move–how to do away with me.

The door opened and the van shook as Ben clambered in behind the wheel. Without speaking, he started the engine, eased past the stationary police cars and headed toward the end of the street.

"What about Tanya and Thunder? How are they getting home?"

"All organized," he said his voice cool. "Scuzz came with me. He'll drive your car and make sure Tanya gets home safely before bringing the car back."

"What did Adams say?"

"What do you think he said? Go and buy your amazing fiancé an ice cream with all the trimmings? He said don't let that infuriating woman of yours out of your sight until you walk her down the aisle and when you go on your honeymoon keep her there until we've cleared up this mess."

I frowned. "And you agreed with him?"

"Yes, I agreed," he said through gritted teeth as he flicked a quick look across at me. "I love you, Kat. I'm scared I'll lose you. And if I have to chain you to the bed until the plane is due to take off for Kangaroo Island to keep you safe…so be it."

Not going to happen.

Although I'd been berating myself for my part in this debacle only moments before, hearing Ben say exactly what I'd been thinking made me prickly. I folded my arms across my chest and scowled. "Just try that and you'll be in so much pain you'll be walking with your legs apart for days after." I sat up straighter. "I can look after myself."

"Is that so?" His frown deepened. "Well you've done a crappy job of it so far."

"Meaning?"

Ben, eyes on the road, hands fisted so tightly around the steering wheel his knuckles were white, let out a cross between a laugh and a snarl. "Meaning there's a maniac out there dead-set on killing you.

Meaning the woman I am going to marry and spend the rest of my life loving and caring for has put her life in danger and because I care enough to want to protect her she's throwing my love in my face."

Oh God, he was right.

I slumped back into the seat and let my anger fizzle like a damp squib. Somewhere over the last few days I'd lost sight of why I was marrying Ben. My soul mate. The love of my life. Too busy acting like Nancy Drew on steroids, I'd barely been thinking of our wedding. Or Ben. If the boot was on the other foot and some depraved murderer was setting his sights on Ben, I'd be the first one to throw myself in the firing line, do anything necessary to protect him. Including locking him up to keep him safe.

I let out a sniff and bit my lip to stop it from trembling. Ben meant far more to me than my stupid pride. My hand found its way across the rough leather of the seat and crept up onto the strong masculine thigh beside me. "I'm sorry," I said wriggling closer and breathing in the familiar smell of fresh air, dogs and the faint smell of the woodsy cologne he'd put on after his shower earlier in the day. While I'd been driving around shopping, tasting cake and pretending to be a sleuth, he'd been hard at it—working the dogs, helping his brother brand calves and getting everything sorted at home so we could take off on our honeymoon without worrying. I sighed. "Sometimes I wonder what you see in me, Ben."

Ben's hand covered mine. "I see a compassionate woman who has a heart bigger than a bull elephant. A woman who cares so much for her friends she puts her own life in danger. An exasperating woman who I sometimes feel like shaking because I don't want to lose her." He squeezed my hand so hard, I winced. "'Cos if I lost you, babe, there'd be no point in me going on."

Wow! Had I hit the jackpot with this guy, or what? Benjamin Taylor, the man I'd let into my life and into my heart. The man who'd soon be my husband—for better or for worse—and how could it not be better? My hand found the warmth of Ben's thigh again as every part of me ached to feel his arms wrapped around me, his naked body on top of mine. Damn. There was no way I could take Ben home with my grandmother's sharp eyes noting every move we made. Too embarrassing. And I couldn't wait until we booked into our honeymoon suite on Kangaroo Island.

Almost panting by now, I dug into the back pocket of my jeans for my mobile and sent off a message to Gran and Fred to let them know I wouldn't be home until the morning and then turned to Ben. "Okay, drive to your place." My hand moved further up his thigh, in exploration mode. "And make it fast. We're either sleeping in your bed tonight or you can pull over and I'll take you right here, right now, in the back of this van."

Ben wriggled beneath my hand. "You'll have me going through the windscreen if you keep that up, babe." His voice was husky as though desire had wrapped her lustful arms around him too but he had the grown-up job of keeping the car on the road. "So…you want to take me right here in the back of the car?"

"If necessary."

"Hmm…as much as that threat makes me hotter than a rooster in a barn yard full of hens, it might be more fun to spend the rest of the night naked and sweaty in the seclusion of my caravan?"

"D'ya still have that king-sized mirror installed over the top of your bed or have you taken it down ready for the big shift?"

"Still there, babe," he said, and let out a long hot breath. "And so is my waterbed."

I couldn't wipe the smile off my face as I thought of that waterbed moving sensually underneath us, it's warm ripples stroking my bare skin. "Well, come on, Benjamin, get a move on. You're driving like an old man of sixty."

Ben slowed down, bit rubber while doing a U turn, and then accelerated in the opposite direction. And when we arrived at Ben's family home, we didn't go into the house to say hello to his Dad or his brother, Nick. We didn't stop to pat the two pet calves that came lolloping over to watch us tumble out of the car. Instead, Ben scooped me up in his arms, kicked open the caravan door and carried me inside.

His mouth, sizzling hot, never left mine as I slid slowly down the length of his body, enjoying the hardness, the evidence of scintillating sex to come, until my feet touched the floor. And when the kiss deepened and his tongue twined around mine, simulating sex, I moaned, my breath catching in my throat. "Gotta get closer." Detaching my lips from his mouth long enough to rip several buttons off his shirt and skim both hands underneath, I moaned again. This was my Ben. With smooth cool skin, rippling muscles and a six pack that would stand up and be counted in any Mr. Universe competition.

Before I could get my fill of tasting every muscle and crevice on his magnificent shoulders and chest, I found myself upended on the bed, minus everything but my socks. Cool air caressed my skin as I stared up into Ben's ceiling mirror. The wanton female stretched out on his bed, legs wide, aching to be touched and kissed and stroked everywhere.

"Oh, babe, you're so beautiful." Ben stood looking down at me, his eyes hungry as they traveled over my body. Like checking the contents of a mouthwatering box of chocolates before plunging in and devouring the lot.

"Get your clothes off," I said in my best schoolmarm voice. "Now!"

Ben's grin was wicked as he kicked off his shoes. "Yes, ma'am."

My mouth dry, I watched Ben perform a slow strip-tease. First one sock came off and landed on the chest-of-drawers, and then the other which he spun in slow circles then flipped in the air. Swaying on the spot, he dragged his shirt over his head and peeked around it before tossing it on the chair. Then, still dancing on the spot to silent music, he undid the zip of his jeans, wriggled until they hit the ground and stepped out of them. Once his jocks joined his jeans he twirled, showing off the muscles in his tight bum. I licked my lips and whistled. "Woohoo! You could get paid to do that routine, Benjamin."

His grin widened further as he knelt on the bed, one lazy finger tracing a circle around my nipple, setting it on fire. "Maybe I should perform a striptease at your hen's party tomorrow night? Give the girls something hot to eyeball."

"And maybe I'll fight every woman there. Blacken their eyes so they can't see you."

"You'd do that?" Eyes hooded, his fingers left my nipple and started their slow tantalizing journey downwards.

"Oh, yeah!" I gasped and squirmed as a bolt of pleasure ripped through me causing all rational thought to scatter like leaves from a blower.

"Does that feel good?" Ben's husky voice whispered in my ear.

Head back, body arched, I was just about to show him exactly how good, when the mood was broken by a loud hammering on the caravan door.

No! No! Not now…

"Go away!" Ben growled. "Unless someone's dying I don't want to know about it."

"Sorry, it's Scuzz on the phone," Ben's brother, Nick, yelled through the closed door. "He wants to talk to Kat. Says she's not answering her phone and Tanya's gone missing."

"Tanya? Missing?" As I unglazed my eyes, shoved Ben off me and sat up, I felt like I'd had a bucket of ice water thrown over me. I scrambled off the bed and reached for an old flannelette robe of Ben's that he'd flung over a nearby chair. "How could Tanya go missing? She was with Scuzz." Tightening the ties around the middle of the robe, I threw open the caravan door and snatched Nick's mobile from his hand. "Scuzz? What do you mean – Tanya's gone missing?" I said slamming the phone to my ear. "She can't have. You drove her home."

"Why did you switch your mobile off?" Scuzz's voice thundered in my ear. "Everyone's worried about you because you weren't answering your phone. And neither is Ben."

I took a deep breath and ignored the question. There was no way I was answering that one. "What's happened to Tanya?"

"Well, I dropped her at her front door, like we arranged and then when I couldn't get through to you to find out if you were safe, I rung Tanya…"

"And?"

"She sounded strange. As though there was someone in the room with her…"

"Go on."

"Well, that's it. In the middle of our conversation she just wasn't there anymore."

I let out a sigh. There was no way Tanya could skull ten beers in fifteen minutes without consequences. This was always par for the course when there was a dead body involved. We'd been through this before. "Scuzz, you saw what Tanya was like when you drove her home. She was dancing around in that pathetic fairy costume, singing rude nursery rhymes. Tanya's drunk. She probably passed out while talking to you and she and her phone are cuddled up together on her lounge room floor."

I looked across at Ben who was still standing naked by the bed, his Love God slowly deflating. I winked and sent him a cheeky smirk, indicating I'd be quite happy to remedy the situation–the moment I sorted out the current misunderstanding.

"So you see Scuzz," I said into the phone, ready to end the conversation quickly and get back to important business. "Tanya might have the headache from hell when she wakes up, but she'll be–"

"Kat," Scuzz broke in. "I'm at Tanya's now. Her front door's open and there's no sign of her inside or outside the house." He cleared his throat and I could almost smell his fear pulsing through the phone lines. "She's gone missing."

A jagged shard of ice skewered my chest while the words 'she's gone missing' reverberated in my brain. Tangled knots twisted around in my stomach. I had to force myself to keep breathing. My eyes found Ben's as I mouthed the words, 'Tanya's gone missing' to him. He nodded and immediately grabbed for his shirt. "Give us ten minutes, Scuzz," I said into the phone. "Ben and I are on our way."

15

Nᴵɴᴇ ᴀɴᴅ ᴀ ʜᴀʟꜰ ᴍɪɴᴜᴛᴇꜱ ʟᴀᴛᴇʀ, Ben's van came to a screeching halt in front of Tanya's gateway. I could see her little red Yaris parked in the driveway and every light on inside the house. Did Scuzz turn on the lights? Or were they like that when he arrived?

A woebegone Petunia, Tanya's normally happy-go-lucky gray Lurcher met us at the front door with her tail jammed between her legs. If Tanya left the door open when she left, why didn't Petunia follow her? Unless Tanya didn't walk out the door under her own steam.

Visibly shaking, the dog peered up at us with those sad confused eyes and her tail gave a few half-hearted wags. Then, realizing she'd found someone she knew, she let out a shrill bark and tried to climb into my arms. An impossible feat. Staggering, as her weight hit me in the chest, I fell back onto Ben who held me up while I pried the sixty-pound dog from around my neck. She didn't know what was going on and seemed to be getting under everyone's feet, so I emptied three cups of kibble into her dish, filled her water bowl and let her out in the backyard.

Gran and Fred had also joined the search. Although way past their bed time, they were both on full alert and according to Fred, 'on a mission'. Scuzz told us the pair of seniors hijacked the Harleys, strapped Fred's walker onto one and refused to let him and Thunder leave without them. How Fred managed to get his frail body onto the pillion and hang onto Scuzz without falling off, I shuddered to think.

There were four empty beer bottles in the trash and another two, unopened, sat on the kitchen table, still in their cardboard container. I closed my eyes. Jesus Tan, what were you thinking? "She's totally smashed," I said and shrugged one shoulder. "Let's look around again. Maybe she'd curled up somewhere, sleeping it off."

We split up and did a more thorough search of the house and back yard, checking every space large enough to hide a sleeping drunk. We checked inside the wardrobes, under the beds, in the cupboards, on the verandah, in the dog kennel, and even inside the large green rubbish bin at the back door. Gran and Fred, working as a team, produced a torch and shone it under the house in case she had crawled under there, couldn't get out, and fallen asleep.

But no Tanya.

Becoming more apprehensive by the minute, Scuzz, Thunder, Ben and I huddled in the middle of Tanya's kitchen. While we discussed what to do next, Gran and Fred decided to make coffee. Coffee sharpened the brain cells, according to Gran. She unearthed a tablecloth from one of Tanya's cupboards to cover the scratched kitchen table then placed six mugs, an open carton of milk and a sugar bowl on top. Fred, not to be outdone, raided the pantry and was now in the process of arranging two packets of Tim Tam biscuits on a floral dinner plate in the middle.

Thunder shook her head when Fred offered her a biscuit, too concerned with tugging her mobile from the back pocket of her leather pants. "I think it's time we informed the police," she said, her ultra-serious cop face telling us she couldn't see any other way around solving Tanya's disappearance.

"You can, but it'll be a waste of time," I told her. "Tanya's an adult. There's no way our local police are going to be interested in her disappearance—especially as she's only been gone for an hour."

"I'm afraid Kat's right, sis," Scuzz said, his voice gruff. He seemed to fill the room with his huge presence as he politely took the plate of biscuits from Fred, passed them around and then deposited the half-empty plate back on the table.

"I realize that, but it wouldn't hurt to let DI Adams know she's missing. You know, in case her disappearance has anything to do with the murders."

My stomach clenched and I worried my bottom lip with my teeth. Of course this had nothing to do with Mary and Peter's murder. Tanya wasn't involved. She knew nothing. All she did was come with us to Peter's house. But for some reason, I couldn't convince my stomach to agree with my head.

"First, we should ring around. Find out if any of Tanya's friends or her ex knows where she is. We don't want to disturb the DI unnecessarily," said Scuzz who'd found a small white jug in Tanya's top cupboard and was happily filling it with milk from the carton before returning the cardboard carton to the refrigerator. A fancy jug Tanya had more than likely received as a wedding gift twelve years ago and forgotten she owned.

"I agree with Scuzz," said Ben, which had Scuzz looking up in surprise from his new job of pouring hot water from the kettle into the mugs. I noticed Gran smiling and nodding her head at the huge tattooed biker like he was the best thing she'd come across since chocolate-covered biscuits. "Who knows?" Ben snitched another Tim Tam from the plate. "Dan could have called in here, seen what a mess Tan was in and taken her back to his place to sleep it off."

"Maybe." Thunder frowned. "But he wouldn't go away and leave the front door open."

"You evidently haven't been introduced to Dan," I said rolling my eyes at her. "Tanya's ex is such a slob it wouldn't enter his head to close the door behind him. He'd leave that to her. And the condition Tan was in, she was probably too busy puking."

"So," put in Fred as he dipped his Tim Tam into his coffee. "We'll take a break, drink our coffee, and then ring Tanya's friends. Right?"

"Got it in one, Fred." I gave Fred's shoulder a squeeze then chose a cup from the row on the table, added milk and sugar and wandered into the lounge room. I needed time to think this through. To be honest, I couldn't see Dan calling in to check on Tanya tonight. Erin would be tucked up in bed by now and although a bad husband, he was a good father. But where else could Tanya have gone? There was no reason to visit a friend. In her condition she couldn't drive–plus her car was still parked in the driveway.

I moved across to my favorite chair, the large saggy armchair in front of the unlit fireplace. Tanya had to be somewhere. She couldn't just disappear like a rabbit from a magician's hat. Placing my coffee cup on the side table next to the chair, I stared down at Sweetie, Tanya's fierce ginger tom cat. Over the years we'd had many a battle over this chair–also his favorite. The slit-eyed cat stared back at me, ginger hair standing on end, back arched and growling low in his throat like an old-time steam train snorting its way out of a station.

Not in the mood to do battle with the-cat-from-hell tonight, I collapsed into an even saggier armchair on the opposite side of the coffee table. Sweetie blinked, shook his head and, evidently not trusting my easy capitulation, curled up facing me. For the next five minutes he continued to eye me off like a bag of fireworks next to a smoker.

"Has anyone checked the tool shed?" said Ben who'd followed me and was now perched on the arm of my chair.

"That was Fred's job," called out Gran from the kitchen.

Fred shook his head. "Nothing in the shed except cobwebs, spiders and umpteen boxes of Tupperware."

Tanya's efforts at hosting Tupperware parties a couple of years ago had resulted in lots of fun and games but very little actual selling. Hence the ten boxes of unsold goods.

"What about her neighbors?" I asked taking a sip of coffee and leaning my head against Ben's arm. "Anyone spoken to them?"

"I did," said Thunder. "The neighbor on the right said he heard Tanya singing on the top of her voice when Scuzz dropped her off, but nothing since. And the neighbor on the right, who was rather cranky about being woken up as I'd also woken the baby, told me how much she hated her day-job, her husband, her kids and especially me and then slammed the door in my face."

I let out a sigh. Tanya's little red Yaris was still parked in the driveway so she hadn't driven anywhere and she wouldn't have been capable of walking any further than the front gate without collapsing face first, laughing at her dilemma, and then passing out. "The car…" I said, suddenly alert. "Has anyone checked to see if Tanya's in her car?"

All eyes turned to Fred. Scratching his head, he screwed up his nose. "Well…I did look through the front window…"

"But did you open both doors and check the inside?" growled Gran walking across and standing over him, arms folded. She had that scary, you're-in-for-it expression on her face I'd seen many times as a child.

Fred was saved from a possible clip over the ear by the sound of voices that appeared to be coming from the front of the house. "Sounds like we have company," he said as he pushed himself up off the seat and shuffled behind his walker, ready for action.

From outside, I heard a loud snort of laughter followed by the sound of the front door opening. Tanya? The murderer and an accomplice exchanging jokes about dead people? I stood up and faced the kitchen doorway. Immediately Ben got to his feet and moved across in front of me. I looked around at my dysfunctional friends and family, all alert, all eyes zeroed in on the kitchen doorway. Waiting. Scuzz and Ben, edgy, muscles twitching, prepared to take on a mob of rotting zombies, if necessary. Thunder, her cop face in place, ready to slap handcuffs on whoever came through the door first. And my eighty-year old Gran brandishing a kettle as a weapon while Fred, her gallant lover and protector, dragged his replica gun from somewhere in his underwear and aimed it at the kitchen door.

"Yoohoo! Anyone in there?"

My mouth slammed open as my sister Liz, dressed in an incongruous black floor-length overcoat, strolled into the kitchen with her ex-con boyfriend, Scott. She grinned at everyone as though she'd seen us all yesterday–instead of six months ago when she and Scott took off for parts unknown. Sleepy-eyed as usual, Scott sported an ancient pair of jeans, a loose white top, suede fringed vest, and thongs. His streaked blonde hair was flattened to his head by an iridescent green and red head-band. Typical hippie.

And held up between them, ready to collapse in a heap if they let her go, was the missing Tanya.

"Where did you find her?" asked Thunder as she and Ben hurried over to rescue Tanya from the couple who'd been virtually dragging her along by the heels. They deposited her in an empty armchair where she gave a sickly grin, closed her eyes, and started to snore.

"Found her in her car," said Liz, with a dismissive shoulder shrug. "Scott and I, we were just swinging down the driveway, you know, getting' ready to say, 'SURPRISE' as soon as you opened the front door, and we heard this strangled moan coming from the back of Tanya's car. 'Twas enough to make me drop me dacks–" She rolled her eyes and stuck her tongue out the side of her mouth. "–if I'd been wearing any. Anyway, Scott opened the car door and there she was. Curled up on the floor, moaning, and looking like she'd been dragged ten miles behind a tractor."

All eyes turned to Fred. "Sorry, sorry," he mumbled, wincing when Gran's fist connected with his shoulder. "I should have opened the doors and checked inside. Difficult when you're toting a walker though."

"But what are you doing here, Liz?"

"And it's wonderful to see you too, sister dear."

"I mean…how did you know we were here…at Tanya's?"

"Jake told us. We rocked up at your place, like, ready to crash for the night." She shrugged one bony shoulder. "No one home–that is, except Jake–and we found him asleep on a chair in the kennel house." As she came closer she started slowly shucking out of her long overcoat. "Any coffee left there, Gran? It's, like, been a long drive down from Mildura. Didn't think we'd make it in time, did we Scott? But hey, the Kombi went like a dream and we arrived with hours to spare." As her coat dropped in a black heap on the floor, Liz stepped away from it and then with both arms outstretched turned to me with a flourish. "Da da! Surprise!"

Playing along, I cut my eyes to her and when the reality of what I saw hit me, did a double-take and gasped, my mouth opening and shutting like a fish out of water. "But-but…Liz…you're pregnant!"

She looked down at the front of her fringed green and orange mini skirt and patted her stomach before raising one eyebrow at me, a grin teasing her lips. "So I am. Ten out of ten for observation. Although–as I'm six months gone–it's sort of hard not to notice."

"Six months? But that means…"

"Right on, big sis. I'm glad you know how to count. Baby Bradly was conceived six months ago, while Scott and I were shacked up in your house."

For a moment all I could think of was the marathon sex that had been going on while Liz and Scott, plus all their weird protestor friends had stayed with me. But that was quickly replaced with an overwhelming feeling of wonder. A baby had been conceived in my house. A baby! My house! I grinned at her. And then the rest of her words finally infiltrated the confusion inside my head. "Baby Bradly?" I didn't think my mouth could fall open any further, but it did. "Does that mean what I think it means?"

Her grin was the same grin she always used to give me when we were growing up. When she surprised me with something she thought was cute–but rarely turned out to be cute at all. "Yep. Scott and I tied the knot–very quietly–two weeks ago."

"You what?"

"Oh, Elizabeth." Gran, who'd been listening with a small grandmotherly smile on her face up until now, stared at her youngest granddaughter with concern. "But where? How?"

Good questions, both of them. Only I'd add another one…why?

My gaze fell on Scott, who'd been very quiet up until now. Earlier in the year I'd saved Scott from certain death when some bad guys knocked him out and threw him in his car, first making sure the windows were up and that a hose went from the exhaust into the car. Maybe I should have kept on walking that day. "And what do you think about being a father, Scott?"

He wrapped one arm around Liz, pulled her against him and the smile he turned on me said it all. It said, thank you for saving my life because now I'm married to a wonderful funny girl, I have a baby on the way and lots to live for. "Can't wait," he said and winked at me. "It's a girl and we've decided to call her Sunshine Katrina Bradly."

I think that's about when I collapsed back on the cat, only to leap out of the chair again as Sweetie let out an earsplitting yowl, and then hissed and bit me on the arm. Ben kissed the bite better before wrapping his arms around me, his grin even wider than Liz and Scott's.

"Come here, Aunty Kat," he said, his eyes alight with mischief as he dragged me up against his granite-hard chest. He looked around at all the smiling faces and punched the air with a closed fist. "Hey!" he said his smile a mile wide. "And I'm going to be baby Sunshine's, Uncle Ben."

"And what about Ma?" I said, exchanging a giggle with Liz. "Queen Boadicea is going to be a grandmother."

Liz shook her head and for a moment she looked a little lost, vulnerable. "I guess Ma, as usual, will be thoroughly pissed off when she finds out."

"No, she won't. I won't let her." Gran clattered across the room and pulled Liz into a big hug. "Your mother will be tickled pink, darling. Just like me." Eyes shining, she turned to Fred and grinned. "Hey, Freddie, I'm going to be a Great-grandmother."

Fred returned her grin with a wickedly suggestive hip wiggle. "And you'll be the sexiest, hottest, great-grandmother in the whole of Resthaven."

I had to smile. Never in a million years would Grandpa Hamilton have given Gran such a compliment. But of course, never in a trillion years would Gran have expected it from him. Fred, on the other hand, was the exact opposite and already, I loved him.

Liz rubbed her stomach in satisfaction and lifted one eyebrow in my direction. "Still want me to be your bridesmaid?"

"You're my only sister. Why wouldn't I?" Uh! Oh! That's when I had a sudden thought and felt my shoulders slump. "The dress!" I yelped. "Your bridesmaid's dress won't fit you. It was modelled on me and I didn't know I had to shove a football under my jeans before the dressmaker took my measurements." I glared at my irresponsible sister and shook my head. "You could have let me know, Liz. What am I going to do now? Your dress will never fit you."

Gran tut-tutted and squeezed my shoulder. "Don't worry, dear. Maybe your dressmaker-lady can unpick the zip and fit a gusset in the back panel. And then, if Liz drapes a wide sash around her middle, no-one will notice the difference."

Liz gave a careless shrug. "Or I can always wear something of my own."

"Noooo!" Both Gran and I shouted at the same time. I put an arm around Liz's shoulders and led her over to the kitchen table, handed her a cup of coffee and indicated a chair for her to sit down, rest her baby bump. "Okay, little sis, here's what's going to happen. I'll take your dress over to Gloria's first thing in the morning and see what she can do. No need to give Ma a heart attack by wearing Birkenstock sandals, hot-pink bell bottoms with fringes and some iridescent red green blue and yellow tie-dyed shirt. Plus, think of the expense. I'd have to issue all my guests with sunglasses just to ward off the glare."

"Ha ha. Very funny." Liz frowned. "This bridesmaid's dress you're talking about better not make me look too normal."

I sighed, let out a noisy breath of frustration. "Don't worry, sister dear. Nothing could ever make you look normal."

Tanya, who'd woken up during the baby discovery, appeared to be getting rather agitated. I could see her wildly beckoning me. Probably needed to puke. So, leaving Liz in Gran's tender care, I wandered across to the bedraggled mess slumped in the armchair. "What's up, Tan? Want me to force-feed you black coffee? Try to sober you up?"

She grabbed me by the arm and pulled me closer so she could hiss in my ear. "Bathroom. Now."

Yep. I was right. We lurched our way to the bathroom at the rear of the house, me gripping one arm to keep her upright, Tanya staggering at every step. "You really must stop drinking yourself into oblivion whenever we find a dead body," I told her as I closed the bathroom door behind us.

"Not my fault," she growled, holding her head in both hands. "I wouldn't have to get myself in such a state if you stopped finding them." Still wearing her overcoat wrapped around her fairy costume, Tanya slumped onto the toilet seat, a picture of misery. If her face was any grayer she'd be stretched out on an undertaker's slab getting fitted for a coffin.

"Look, what say I dig up fresh clothes for you? That fairy costume might look cute on an eight-year-old, but…" I wrinkled my nose to show her exactly how un-cute white tulle, gossamer wings and sparkles looked on a bombed-out twenty-eight-year-old mother. "And maybe have a shower?" I suggested. The stink of booze was making my eyes water.

"Um…" she said and blinked up at me.

I sighed. It was like talking to an empty box of tissues. "Honestly, Tan, you'll feel much more comfortable in your jeans or your trackies."

"Nah…" She blinked again and began fumbling around inside the pockets of her overcoat.

As I checked out my reflection in her bathroom mirror, I ran a hand through my disheveled hair, cleaned my teeth with my tongue and then, squinting closer, noted the deep ruts trailing from the corners of my eyes. Ugh! How I hated magnified mirrors that exaggerated every flaw. Retailers should be banned from selling them on the grounds they have a 99% possibility of causing depression. I looked away. If I didn't get Tanya cleaned up soon, she'd end up passing out. Kneeling on the bathroom floor, beside her, I tried again. "What if I help you get into your pajamas and tuck you into bed," I said and grinned. "Hey, I'll even read you one of Erin's old Dr. Seuss books and stay with you until you drop off to sleep."

She shook her head, both hands still fumbling in the pockets of her bedraggled overcoat. "I have something to show you. Found it on the floor in Peter's kitchen when I dropped the beer can."

"You took something from the crime scene? Oh my God, DI Adams will throw the book at you." I stared at my best friend and shook my head. "Why?"

She tugged something out of a pocket inside her black coat and, hand shaking, eyes not leaving mine, held it up for me to see. "That's why."

I felt my breath whoosh from my chest as I stared, disbelievingly at the object lying in the flat of Tanya's palm.

"It's – it's…"

"Your engagement ring."

"But how? Why?"

"Jules is in custody, so no way could the police blame her for Peter's death. Looks like it was your turn to be framed." She handed the ring to me and grinned. "But not now. Not without the evidence."

16

Thoughts kept spinning around in my head.

Why me? And how did my ring end up as part of a crime scene? After the dumpster debacle at the dog track, I'd placed my ring on the coffee table in my lounge room as a reminder to take it to the jewelers to be altered. But with all that was going on, I forgot. So, the killer–he or she–must have entered my house, spotted the ring and slipped it into their pocket, fully intending to frame me for their next crime. Just like with Jules' gun.

But I'd muddied their plans by visiting Peter that night.

Even if Tanya hadn't spotted my ring when she bent to pick up a dropped beer-can and even if the police had discovered it, the murderer's plan wouldn't have worked. 'Cos the ring could have fallen off my finger when I squatted down beside Peter's body to see if I could help.

Friday morning. Twenty-four hours to my wedding. I'd left Tanya snoring louder than a helicopter in full flight and arrived home around 5am. I'd showered and changed into my working clothes of faded jeans, rubber boots, and a shapeless purple sweater, two-sizes too big for me, then, with a slice of toast smothered in marmalade jam and a hot milky cup of coffee inside me, tossed up whether to wake the newly-weds and the oldies with a morning coffee. It was a no-brainer really. They needed their sleep. Plus, I'd hate to walk in on an early-morning game of pass-the-lubricant.

As I wandered down the path toward the kennel-house to let the racing dogs out into long-runs and prepare their breakfast, I could see a near-naked man stretched out on the ground up ahead, doing push-ups. It was Ben. Fascinated, I leaned against a huge pepper tree that provided shade to the kennels in summer, intent on enjoying the view. And what a view it was. Ben was wearing nothing but a pair of faded shorts and scuffed R.M.Williams boots. His tight well-honed muscles strained to the max and sweat rolled off his naked chest and trickled between his six-pack abs with each push-up. All indicating he'd been going at it for a while.

"Well, well," I said coming up behind him as he counted out his one-hundred-and-tenth push-up. "Someone's feeling antsy."

He flopped on the ground and let out a long moan. "Jesus, Kat, I think I'm going to die right here and now. You might have to scrape me up off the cement and drip me into a wooden box for burial."

"Couldn't sleep, hey?"

He rolled over onto his back. Arms and legs splayed, he looked up at me, one eyebrow quirking. "Impossible. Every time I closed my eyes this hot sexy babe popped into my caravan."

"And…"

"And she stripped, oh-so-slowly. One item of clothing at a time until all she had left on was a shocking red garter belt. Hell, by then I was panting so much…I almost swallowed my tongue.'

"Yeah?"

"And then she began to sway, you know, from side to side with her hands running up and down her body and her eyes inviting me to lick every inch of her hot naked skin."

Oh boy! "And did you?"

"Hoo yeah! And the way she moaned and screamed my name when she came…"

Mouth dry, breath ragged, I ran my tongue over my lips and squirmed, feeling sudden dampness between my legs. "That hot sexy babe in your dreams better have been me, buster."

He slowly climbed to his feet and slung one arm around my shoulders, his warm breath blowing in my ear. "Sure was, babe. So, how about we find somewhere quiet and finish off what we started last night?"

I closed my eyes and steadied my breathing. "Tempting," I whispered. "But nah, you're too sweaty–"

"I'll wipe myself off with a towel."

"I'd die of embarrassment if someone walked in on us."

Ben threw back his head and let out a long breath. "And I'll die of frustration if we have to wait until our honeymoon."

"Come on, Tiger," I said grabbing Ben's hand and leading him through the kennel-house door. "Best cure for sexual frustration is to work it off."

"Ha," he snorted. "Why do you think I was killing myself by doing push-ups when you arrived?"

"Not long now and you'll have me completely to yourself. To do whatever you desire." I laughed up at him, then, remembering Tanya's discovery, bit my bottom lip. "That's if I live that long."

"What you talking about?"

I hadn't filled Ben in on Tanya's sleight of hand. Not yet. Last night, with everyone milling around Tanya's kitchen, laughing and celebrating Liz's good news, I decided to keep it quiet. After all, I could just imagine Thunder's reaction to Tanya removing evidence from a crime scene and even Fred would have insisted we ring DI Adams and put him in the picture. And they were both probably right. But I couldn't drop Tanya in the middle of this. Bad enough I'd removed the threatening note from Peter's office.

I bit down harder on my bottom lip, fisted my hands at my side before speaking. "I think someone's trying to frame me for Peter's murder."

"Why?" Ben, who'd dragged a towel from the pile on top of a cupboard inside the dog shed, looked up from wiping sweat from his chest. He frowned across at me, his eyes dark and concerned and with that full-on protection thing going on. Like he'd beat up anyone who tried to hurt me. But for some reason, this made me want to cry. His eyes bored into mine. "Okay, Kat, spill it. What have you got yourself into this time?"

By now, the dogs were in full throttle, barking, jumping up at their gates, tossing their bedding in the air. I had to shout to be heard over the din. "I'll explain after we've let the dogs into the outside yards. Okay?"

He grunted and threw his towel in the direction of the treatment table before shaking his head at me. "I sometimes think I should employ a full-time nanny–just to keep you out of trouble."

I tossed a handful of leads at him and then opened the door of the first kennel. "Do that, Benjamin, and you'll really know the meaning of frustration."

By the time all the dogs were out in their appropriate yards and I'd produced two buckets of warm soapy water, squirted in a good dollop of disinfectant and hitched a couple of mops down from the drying rack behind the door, I was in control again.

"Well?" said Ben looking quite cute, shirtless. He'd already straightened the bedding in the first kennel and was wielding a mop like a pro.

I let out a sigh as I looked across at the hunky guy with the mop. I was so lucky. I had a soon-to-be husband I adored. A kennel full of dogs that tried their heart out for me on the track. And family and friends who, although madly dysfunctional, appeared to love me.

But thinking about my engagement ring in the flat of Tanya's palm–the ring she'd found on the floor of Peter's kitchen–I was finding it hard to breathe.

I stuck my mop in the bucket, squeezed the excess water out through the roller and began washing the cement floor in Lofty's kennel. "It's these murders, Ben. I'm scared."

Ben was beside me almost before I'd finished talking. "Babe, the murders have nothing to do with you," he said, lifting my chin with one finger and kissing me on the nose. "Forget them. Let the police do their job. You've got enough to worry about with getting that screwball family of yours onto the beach at Semaphore at the crack of dawn tomorrow." He grinned and the crinkles around his eyes deepened.

"You know, I'm actually looking forward to seeing whether your oddball uncle turns up drunk or not and if your Ma arrives toting a large pair of scissors in her Mother-of-the-bride handbag." His grin widened. "And I'm glad you've arranged for our wacky wedding to be videoed, 'cos our future kids wouldn't believe us, without proof."

"But there's something else." Reluctant to spoil his cheer-Kat-up mood, I sucked in a deep breath and let it all out in one rushed statement. "Whoever killed Peter stole my engagement ring with the express purpose of framing me for his murder."

That put a slight dampener on proceedings. By the time I'd brought Ben up to date with the latest episode in the murder saga, both Jake and Scuzz had arrived, been told of the threatening note plus the intent to frame me and the three of them had decided, without any input from me, to tag me until Ben and I were on the plane heading for Kangaroo Island. In other words, I wasn't allowed out of their sight until I was safely ensconced in my seat belt on the plane.

No amount of common-sense narrative, discussions on the fact that I was an adult and therefore they had no control over me, made a scrap of difference. The consensus was that until I was safely in the plane, wherever I went, I'd have a tagger. In fact, the moment Thunder poked her nose into the dog shed she was roped in as a co-jailer, along with Gran and Fred who suggested I be locked in my room until the wedding car arrived the following morning to take me to the ceremony.

Grrrr...

So...it wasn't until 10am that I remembered to ring the dressmaker about adding an insert to the back of Liz's bridesmaid dress. She told me to bring Liz and the dress straight over and she'd do what she could in the short time available but couldn't promise anything.

Fair enough. If Liz had to wear the dress with the zip undone all the way down the back and her bare skin showing through, it was entirely her own fault for not letting me know about the baby bump.

I stomped up the stairs and banged on my bedroom door. "Liz," I yelled. "Get up! The dressmaker's agreed to alter your dress but you have to come with me to get it fitted."

No answer.

I banged again. Harder this time. "Liz. Scott. I'm coming in. The dress has to go now or there's no way it'll be ready in time for the wedding tomorrow."

By now Gran, whose beady eyes had been following me ever since I walked in the front door, had climbed the stairs and stood beside me, arms folded over her chest. "Elizabeth Jennifer McKinley, if you don't open this door in exactly ten seconds I'm going to come in and upend a bucket of water over you."

The door opened and a tousled headed Scott, wearing pajama bottoms only, blinked out at us. "Sorry, guys. Liz's feeling a bit cranky today. She says the dress will have to go to the dressmakers without her." He wiped sleep from his eyes with the back of one hand and opened his mouth in a jaw-stretching yawn that reeked of garlic. "Liz's been in and out of the bathroom all night. Kept us both awake." He yawned again but this time I was quick to step out of range. "Just one of the joys of pregnancy, according to the doctor. Anyway, she says if you want her to be a bridesmaid tomorrow–she needs to stay in bed today."

Oh, great! Just flippin' great! How was Gloria supposed to alter the garment without Liz's presence?

Gran, radiating authoritarian vibes with every step, pushed past Scott and bustled into the room. "Well, in that case, Elizabeth," she said addressing the hollow-eyed Liz who was slumped on the side of the bed looking like pregnancy was as much fun as poking yourself in the eye with a stick, "we'll take your measurements and give them to the dressmaker." She turned to me. "Go get a tape measure, Katrina, and while you're there, we'll need paper and a pen."

When I returned, a rather disgruntled Liz stood beside the bed, arms stretched to the side. And within seven minutes, Gran had her measurements down on paper, the bridesmaid's dress slung over her arm, and was heading out to the car, me following along behind.

Apparently, it was Gran's turn to tag me while I drove Liz's dress to the dressmakers.

17

"Come in, come in." While Gran and I eased ourselves out of the car, Gloria, all smiles, stood at the front door of her hundred-year-old dwelling and waved us inside.

Constructed back when houses were built to last centuries instead of mere years, the solid stone home with attached front verandah looked as inviting as its smiling owner. Gloria had spent quite a bit of money lovingly modernizing her historic property. As well as a new roof, fresh paint and lots of contemporary additions, she was obsessed with flowers. Even the verandah was a kaleidoscope of color with at least twenty hanging baskets and a window box at both front windows. To me, it looked more like an exhibit at the Chelsea Garden Show than a regular Australian verandah.

"Hi Gloria. Sorry to give you to all this extra work. I feel awful. It's just that my darling sister neglected to let us know she was six months' pregnant."

"Is that normal for her?" she said holding the front door open with one hand while pushing strands of her long dark hair away from her face with the other.

Liz? Normal? I shrugged and rolled my eyes.

Gloria squinted at the car, evidently checking for the other occupant. "Um…is your sister coming?"

"No, and I know this makes it more difficult for you, but Liz is having a bad day." I nodded as if I knew what I was talking about. "She's suffering from pregnancy problems, you see. But, hey, Gran took Liz's measurements, so I hope that's enough." I stopped, indicated my grandmother who, although a little stooped under the weight of the bridesmaid's dress had insisted on carrying it in. "Sorry, Gloria, this is my grandmother, Mrs. Hamilton. Ma's mother."

"Lovely to meet you Mrs. Hamilton. And don't worry, the measurements should be enough–as long as you're not expecting me to make major alterations to the dress."

"Oh, no," said Gran slipping past Gloria and entering the house with me hot on her heels. "Just do what you can in a difficult situation, dear. It's extremely kind of you to help out like this at such short notice."

Following us in, Gloria closed the front door behind her and then led us down a long narrow passageway into her workroom at the rear of the house. A room full of colorful fabrics, original garments in various stages of completion, a state-of-the-art industrial sewing machine and one of those handy dressmaker's models. She shoved a pile of colorful magazines and a heavy roll of tweed material to the far side of a long table next to a couple of notepads a bottle of glue, several reels of different colored cotton thread and a pair of scissors, before taking Liz's dress from Gran and laying it out on the table. "Your granddaughter tells me her wedding gown was originally yours," Gloria said to Gran. "I'm not surprised. You can't find material like this anymore."

Gran's eyes went soft as she appeared to be remembering her own wedding, all those years ago. "After tomorrow, my dress will have been worn by three brides."

Gloria smiled in acknowledgement and rubbed her hands together. "Now, before you go, would you like me to put the kettle on for a cuppa?"

"No, no, can't stay, Gloria. I'm sure you have lots to do and so do we. But, hey, just give me a call when you finish Liz's dress and I'll come and pick it up. And once more, I can't thank you enough." I dug into my jacket pocket and produced the slip of paper with Liz's measurements. "I'll just leave these on the table here beside the dress, shall I?"

"No worries, that'll be fine, Kat." Gloria's eyes were on Gran who'd wandered over to the other side of the workroom to inspect a gorgeous creation currently pinned on Gloria's dressmaker's model. It was a beautiful silk dress, a rich shade of purple, trimmed with a lighter shade of mauve lace.

Gran stroked the material, almost reverently. "This is exquisite, Gloria. Is it for you?"

"Hardly," she snapped. "I have no use for party dresses. It's for a well-heeled client whose husband is taking her somewhere special for their two-week wedding anniversary." For a second Gloria's lips twisted in what could only be envy and then she recovered her composure, pushed her long hair back over her shoulders and forced her lips into a caricature of a smile. I was tempted to rush over and give the woman a hug but knew she'd only push me away, furious at my sympathy.

"You're so young, dear," said Gran, also picking up on Gloria's hostility. "Certainly not past wearing pretty party dresses. In fact, I think this color would suit you."

"Huh. No time for frippery." Gloria scowled and headed for the workroom door. As she passed the long table she tidied the bottle of glue and notebooks behind the stack of magazines and ran her hand reverently over the large roll of tweed material. There was no second-guessing–she didn't want to talk anymore and we'd outstayed our welcome. "I'll get straight onto the alterations and ring you when the dress is ready," she said over her shoulder. "It should only take me two or three hours."

Gran and I followed Gloria's stiff back along the passageway to the front door. There were no smiles on leaving. Instead, the moment we passed through, the door closed behind us.

Gran stood on the verandah, shaking her head in bewilderment. "What did I say?"

"You said nothing, Gran. It's not you." I shrugged and headed for the car. "I just think Gloria's been badly hurt by a man at some time in her life and it's made her very bitter. Come on, let's go home and I'll make you one of my famous cappuccinos with a dollop of brandy and sprinkled with cinnamon. It'll not only grow hairs on your chest– you'll be shaving a beard off your chin by morning."

Gran laughed and settled herself into the passenger seat beside me. "In that case, maybe you should concoct one of your famous brews for Gloria, when you come back to pick up Liz's dress."

"Maybe another time. Gloria's love life might be up the creek without a life-jacket, but hey, the woman's a marvelous dressmaker and that's all we need today."

It was only a fifteen-minute drive home, but Gran managed to fit three phone calls in on the way. The first to Fred, to remind him to take the chops out of the freezer for tonight's tea. The second to someone by the name of Flora, who I gathered from the conversation was a close friend from Resthaven Retirement Village. And the third, a lengthy tirade to Uncle Tony. For a woman in her eighties, who'd only discovered mobile-phones a few months ago when a salesman with unlimited patience ventured into their aged care residence, she'd become a real pro. Even used it to tell the time and check on the weather.

"Good news, Katrina, your friend, Jules, has been freed on bail," she told me after the last call ended. "Evidently your Uncle Tony's boss stormed the precinct an hour ago and accomplished in three minutes what my inept and lazy son couldn't manage in three days."

"Yay!" I punched the air. Jules out? Jules free to be a bridesmaid at my wedding? I sat up straighter in my seat as another thought occurred to me. "But do the police still think Jules shot Mary Parker?"

"Seems like it. Finding your friend's gun at the crime scene makes it difficult to prove otherwise."

"But it was planted there." Why couldn't the police see that? "Jules was set up–just like the killer tried to frame me."

"We know that, dear, but now it's up to her lawyer to prove it." Gran shook her head as I banged the steering wheel with one hand. "And it doesn't do your friend any good for you to get upset. She'll need you to stay calm and responsible. And be there ready to listen to her vent."

Gran was right. "At least they can't pin Peter's murder on her."

"No, but according to Tony, the police are treating the deaths as two separate murders by two different perpetrators."

"That's rubbish!" I fisted my hands on the steering wheel and let out a soft curse. "Are the cops blind–or just dumber than a bag of spuds? Maybe I should go and give DI Adams a blast. Although I guess it's his boss, D.C.I. Stevens who's behind this. That guy is so self-possessed, so caught up on his looks and worrying if every strand of hair is sitting smugly in place, he can't see past his Grecian nose. Anyone with only one eye open can see the same person killed both Mary and Peter. Why? I don't know. Who? I don't know. But if we can't find the real culprit soon, Jules could find herself locked up for life–for something she didn't do."

"I know, dear." Gran's voice was soothing, placating. "But you can't get involved any more than you already are." She reached across and her soft fingers squeezed my arm.

"But Gran–"

"Listen, darling, you're getting married to a lovely man in the morning. He's worried sick about you getting hurt, or worse. Let's just leave it at that, shall we?"

I bit back another curse. Gran was right. Well, sort of. I could see why Ben was worried about me. Already I'd received a threatening note and the sender had tried to frame me for murder. And yes, I was scared that I could be next on his or her hit-list. So scared, in fact, if I really thought about it too closely, I'd probably wet myself.

But Jules was my friend. I tried to relax my tight shoulder muscles by lifting them up to my ears and back half a dozen times as I drove. Didn't work. I took a deep breath and counted to ten as I exhaled. So…if the situation was reversed and I was the one charged with murder, what would my friend, Jules, do? She'd kick butt, that's what she'd do.

But whose butt?

I let out a sigh. If I knew the answer to that question I'd gather my team together and plan an attack. Tanya would be right beside me–or behind me. Thunder…well, maybe, as long as there was no break-and-enter involved. And I knew both Ben and Scuzz were masters at kicking butt. Maybe even Fred could use his walker as a weapon.

But, of course, I was no closer to knowing who was behind the murders than I was on Wednesday, inside that foul-smelling dumpster. When my hand reached out and touched Mary Parker's cold flesh.

Five minutes later, as we neared my gateway, I could see my good friend, Scuzz – did he ever dress in anything but black leather – holding the gate open for us to pass through. There were six excited GAP dogs, on leads, beside him.

"Hello there, Theodore," Gran called out through the open window. "Are you coming or going with your team of dogs?"

"Good morning, Mrs. Hamilton." Scuzz, his craggy bearded face crinkling in kindness, closed one eye in a conspiratorial wink. "I took the gang for a promenade to the end of the road and back."

"Oh, you're such a good boy. I'm sure the dogs will love you for that, dear."

I put my hand over my mouth to hide my grin. Scuzz, his facial piercings sparkling in the sun, his conspicuous black leather jacket proclaiming him to be a big bad Red Devil, looked so cute when he blushed. "Um…thank you," he said looking down at his size twenty biker boots. "This lot were frolicking in the sand-pit all morning, digging holes and playing chasey, so I thought a little stroll might see them curl up and sleep for the remainder of the day." Hands clutching six leads, he used his powerful tree-trunk sized leg to close the gate behind us. "Katrina, would you like me to bath Lofty, Lucky, Yolo and Tater now? They need to be looking their best when they walk down the aisle with your bridal party."

"Oh, my God, I'd forgotten all about the dogs!" What else had I forgotten? I'd probably think of something I'd missed, while sitting in the bridal car, surrounded by lace and white satin, on the way to Semaphore beach tomorrow morning. "Thank you, Scuzz. That'd be a huge help."

Scuzz tut-tutted. A rare sight to witness from a seven-foot, ginger-bearded member of the Red Devils. "I almost forgot. I have news for you, Katrina. Good news. Your Ma received a phone call from Jules' lawyer while you were away. He said they've released her from jail."

"Great, isn't it? Uncle Tony was just on the phone to Gran. He told us."

"But did he tell you the police have arrested someone else for Mary Parker's murder."

No! Uncle Tony forgot to mention that! "Did he say who?"

"Patti Murdoch. Know her?"

I blinked. "Yes, I know Pattie." I whooshed out a breath. No wonder she'd been so upset at the supermarket yesterday. "But if Pattie killed Mary, how did she manage to steal the guns from Jules? And does she actually know how to use a gun?" I really couldn't see Patti as a cold-blooded killer–and yet who knew what anyone was capable of when put under pressure?

"Oh, I almost forgot," said Scuzz, gathering the leads together ready to walk the dogs back to their GAP quarters. "Your Ma wants to see you. Something about the marquee in the back paddock."

Oh, crap! What now?

"You know," said Gran as we drove down the driveway and stopped the car in front of my chocolate-box house. "For a hulking, tattooed, real scary dude, that man is really quite sweet."

I grinned at her and shook my head. "I don't know what you've done with my old Gran but hey, I reckon the new model is a hundred times better." After exchanging hugs, I placed both my hands in prayer mode and placed them under my chin. "Now, I don't suppose you could wave a magic wand over Ma, could you? Get her to let her hair down and lighten up?"

"Sorry, dear," she said, undoing her seat-belt and letting out a sigh. "I'm afraid your mother wandered into a crater of vinegar years ago and hasn't been able to find her way out since."

"Did you know she told Liz and me about Aunty Sharon being our birth mother?"

"Aah. Finally. I hope you both took it well."

"As well as expected, I suppose. But I must admit it was a relief in a way, to find out why Ma is the way she is."

Gran sighed. "Your mother is a good woman under that brusque exterior but she's had to put up with a lot of disappointments in life. I'm not disparaging your father, dear, but what Helen needs now is a man like my Freddy. A man who can show her how much happier life can be when you learn to laugh."

At that moment, the man who'd taught my Gran how to laugh, came zipping out the front door, his walker breaking the sound barrier as he approached the car, a huge grin deepening the wrinkles in his face. "Hey, girls, you've missed all the fun. It's like a three-ring circus out there in the back paddock. Half a dozen guys are trying to put up this enormous tent and your Ma is running around like a chook with its head chopped off. She's telling them it's supposed to be in the front paddock and they're insisting they've been instructed by the caterers to erect the marquee in the back paddock. Anyway, she has this posh clipboard in her hand and she's wearing the largest straw hat I've ever seen." He grabbed a quick breath. "Hey, it's all coming together now, Kitty-Kat. Can't back out now. There's all these chairs and tables stacked up ready to go inside the tent when and if it eventually goes up and buckets of fresh flowers and colorful banners and all manner of things to make your wedding breakfast the best breakfast in the history of the world."

I grinned at Fred whose eyes were as excited as a kid of ten on his way to his first football match. Funnily enough, my dad used to call me Kitty-Kat when I was a little girl. Once again it hit me and I wished my father was alive and walking me down the aisle in the morning instead of crazy Uncle Tony.

Gran was eyeing Fred off with a speculative glint in her eyes. "Did you remember to take the chops from the freezer?"

Fred shook his head. "There's been far too much excitement around here today to worry about chops, my girl. We'll order a pizza with the lot, extra anchovies, and have the chops when our world's at peace again."

"Says who?"

"Now, now, don't go all frosty on me, Veronica. Come on, let's see you wiggle that cute derriere of yours. Show me the beautiful girl I love." He clapped his hands together. "You know, I haven't had so much fun since the day we went to the Royal Show together and got lost inside the Hall of Mirrors."

"And you won me a cupie doll on one of the sideshows." Gran's let out a loud belly laugh. "Doll's head fell off before we even left the showgrounds." Her arm snaked out and tugged Fred closer. "You know, Frederick, you're the cherry on top of my ice cream. Just keep telling me how much you love me and how beautiful I am and eventually the last of my frost will melt clean away." She lifted her head. "Come here, big boy, and plug your lips into mine."

I gave a little cough to remind them of my presence. But the only response was a tightening of Fred's arms around Gran's waist and some rather juicy sucky sounds as the kisses grew hotter.

"Excuse me, guys, but I'm still here…"

Gran began undoing the buttons on Fred's shirt as she angled her mouth for greater suction. Immediately Fred moaned and I watched his hands leave Gran's waist and slide down over her bottom in an attempt to hitch her up higher.

La la la.

I debated whether I should grab Fred and hold him steady–his skinny chicken-legs looked in danger of collapsing under the extra weight–but the moment his hand disappeared under Gran's skirt, threatening to incinerate the optic nerves in both my eyes, I opted to leave them be.

Eyes glued shut, I sidled away from the two gray-haired lovebirds and then headed in the direction of the back paddock. Ma had worked so hard to make sure my wedding was perfect it was only fair to spend the rest of the day helping her. First, I'd check all was in readiness for both the wedding ceremony and our breakfast reception afterward…

And then I'd get all dressed up ready for tonight's Hen's party–my last night of being single.

18

It was around 1.30am, Saturday morning, before my Hen's party finally wound down. The musicians in The Calendar Guys' band packed up their equipment and the giggly hens straggled out of the local pub to waiting taxis, husbands or boyfriends. And as previously arranged, my closest friends and family all headed for my house. The wedding ceremony was scheduled for sunrise so we planned to spend the next two and a half hours giving each other facials, massages and preparing for my Big Day in a 'girly' environment.

Once home, the first item on my agenda was a long hot bath, complete with half a bottle of bubbles. Then, feeling so relaxed I was in jeopardy of dropping off to sleep, I settled down in front of my bedroom mirror while Rosa, the local hairdresser who'd also attended the Hens' party and was now our personal hairdresser, began working on my hair. Trouble was–whenever I get my hair done it makes me even sleepier. Soothing fingers working rhythmically in my scalp, the way the comb tugs gently at my hair, the smell of hair products that assail the nostrils. Yawn. By the time my hair was looking as good as Rosa could make it I was battling to keep myself from snoring.

Desperately needing air, I wandered outside. The half-moon, high in the sky, was eyeballing me with a Mona Lisa smile on its face. It appeared to be saying: life's pretty good for you, Katrina. You have a great guy, a great future, and you're surrounded by great friends.

And the shadow of a murderer wasn't hanging over me like a bad smell any more. Patti Murdoch, Mary's killer was locked up in the City Watch-house.

But the police were still treating Peter's murder as a separate case, a robbery gone wrong.

Slightly unsettled, I kicked at the gravel under my feet and then took a deep breath, filling my lungs with crisp night air. I shivered. Freaking cold night air. Why didn't I grab a coat before coming outside?

Rubbing at the goosebumps on my arms, I turned to walk back in the house to join the others for more girl-talk, preferably over several strong sobering cups of black coffee, when my mobile chirped its tinny rendition of Can't Stop the Feeling. I frowned. Who would be ringing me at two-thirty in the morning? Surely not the caterers with some last-minute wedding disaster. Or maybe it was Ben, in need of some stimulating phone sex. Smiling, I edged the phone from my pocket and then perched on the small brick wall that separated the front porch from the gravel path.

Hmm…not the caterers and it wasn't Ben's number that lit up my screen.

"Kat, this is Gloria here."

"Gloria?" I blinked, my mind still on having phone sex with Ben.

"Your dressmaker. You haven't picked up your sister's bridesmaid dress."

I closed my eyes and swore under my breath.

"I did ring you earlier but then another rushed job came in which I've been working on all night and I suddenly realized the dress was still hanging up in my workroom."

"I'm so sorry, there's just been so much going on, I forgot all about it," I wailed. "And my wedding ceremony starts in a couple of hours."

"Well, I'll be here working for another hour. What do you want to do?"

"Can I drive over and pick the dress up now?"

"Okay, I'll switch the front light on for you."

The moment I finished the call, my first thought was to jump in the car and head straight to Gloria's. I'd be back with the dress before they'd miss me inside. And then common sense, something I hadn't shown much of in the past, won out. It was 2.30 in the morning. Was Peter's death really a robbery gone wrong? Was Patti really a murderer? And besides, I needed to go inside and grab a coat first.

Tanya and Jules both offered to drive over and pick Liz's dress up for me. As Jules said, this was my wedding day and I should be getting massages, facials and my nails done, not driving around the countryside doing my sister's dirty work. Thunder, from under the hair-dryer, said I should wake Princess Elizabeth up and send her off to pick up her own dress.

Okay, they were probably right but I knew relaxing with a massage or a facial would send me off to sleep and then I'd be all snarly when it came time to walk down the aisle. "No, I'll go. Liz hasn't had her hair done yet and I really need to thank the dressmaker for going beyond the call of duty. Not only has she made four new dresses, altered Gran and Ma's wedding dress to fit me, she's also altered Liz's bridesmaid dress at the last minute and reminded me I need to collect it before the ceremony starts," I told them. "Plus, I'm jumpy. It's not every day a girl gets married, you know. I need to do something proactive or I'll either go to sleep or crawl up the walls like a deranged house-fly high on pesticide."

As Jules was in the middle of a facial, Tanya swallowed the last dregs of her coffee and pushed herself out of the kitchen chair. "Hang on, I'll come with you," she said as she lifted a packet of chocolate biscuits from the kitchen table before grabbing her jacket from the back of the settee. Tater, Lucky and Yolo also offered to accompany me but I reminded them that if they were to look their best when leading the bridal party down the aisle, they needed their beauty sleep.

Tanya and I chattered non-stop on the drive to Gloria's house. Somehow, probably because of the time of the day when most people were sound asleep, and the excitement in the air, it felt like we were off on another one of our adventures. And we'd shared plenty of those over the years. Some good. Some so frightening we were lucky to come through unscathed. Would things be the same once I was married? Or would the fact of me being part of a couple spoil Tanya and my relationship?

"Ben's not like that," Tanya assured me when I put the question to her. "He's the most un-clingy or needy man I know. And hey, he knows better than to try to influence our friendship."

"You're right." I sent her a quick grin. "Not only would he find himself locked out of the bedroom, his white shirts would all mysteriously end up in the washing machine with a set of new bright pink sheets."

Gloria' house lay on the outskirts of Two Wells and at 2.50 in the morning the road was pitch black. It was like driving through a tunnel or a smothering pea-souper fog. I found the only way to see where I was going was to press my nose against the windscreen and squint. No moon and no street lights to help out. The earlier smiley half-moon was now sulking behind a cluster of dark clouds and of course street lights were non-existent on country roads.

"Geez, I hope Gloria remembered to leave her front light on or we're stuffed," I told Tanya as I drove slowly along the road, feeling my way by the car's headlights.

"There it is," she yelled, her head stuck out the passenger side window. "Up ahead."

Thank you, Gloria.

Wriggling my shoulders, which felt tighter than a row of soldered-in screws, I blew out a sigh of relief and headed toward the pin prick of light. I was cutting it fine. There'd be no hanging around. I'd grab the dress, promise the dressmaker a huge bonus and then Tanya and I would head for home. Hopefully I'd still have plenty of time to make myself beautiful and get decked out in my wedding finery–all so I could say, 'I do' to my gorgeous fiancé, Ben.

A small sconce light glowed amber beside Gloria's front door as I slowed to a halt and parked outside the dressmaker's home–but the inside of the house was in complete darkness. Strange. Surely, she hadn't gone to bed. It was only twenty minutes since she'd rung.

"No need to come in with me," I told Tanya as I switched off the engine. "I'll just grab the dress and come straight back out again." I grinned at her and wiggled my hips. "We have a wedding to get dressed-up for and my groom won't be happy if I'm late."

Tanya flung the passenger side door open and hopped out of the car. "Nah, I'll come in with you. It's creepy out here and anyway, I need to clear my head. I might have had one too many wines tonight and I'm not really over last night's beer-fest."

"That's why I settled on one glass of wine and a gallon of orange juice. Wouldn't want to say 'I do' to the wrong guy." I laughed as I closed the car door behind me and followed Tanya through Gloria's front gate and up onto the verandah. "And by the way, you were right, Tan. The Hens loved their gift packs. Even my Gran thought the fruit-flavored condoms were a cute touch."

"Told you so." Tanya lifted her fist to knock on the front door and as she did so, the door creaked open at her touch. She dropped her hand to her side and blinked. "It's open." She frowned across at me. "Why would she leave her front door open at this time of the morning?"

I shrugged one shoulder.

"What'll we do? Go in – or shall I knock?"

I stared at the open door, not quite comfortable with going inside the house without an invite. Gloria was my dressmaker–not a close friend. "Better try knocking first."

Tanya gave a couple of hard raps on the door but there was no answer. "Well?"

"Gloria?" I called out and nudged the door open wider. "It's me, Kat. I've come to pick up Liz's bridesmaid's dress." From the weak light on the verandah, I could just make out what appeared to be several suitcases stacked in the passageway, near the front door. Gloria hadn't said anything about going away on holiday, but I guess with all the work she'd been doing lately, she decided to have a break. Tentatively, I poked my head through the doorway and called out again. "Gloria? You awake in there?" There was no answer and the inside of the house looked far from inviting. In fact, it was almost as black as the bottom of a coal mine.

"Maybe she's fallen over and hit her head."

"But why switch the lights off?"

"I dunno." Careful of her newly styled hair, Tanya rubbed the back of her neck. I could see by her body language that she, like me, had misgivings about leaving the safety of the verandah and venturing into the dark house. "Perhaps she's gone for a walk to stretch her legs?" My best friend's tone was hopeful, as though she really really hoped for the latter and that Gloria would come skipping along the track any minute, greet us with a smile and then go inside and switch on all the lights.

I palmed the door wider and took a step inside. Immediately the hairs on the back of my neck stood on end. Something felt wrong, but as Tanya said, Gloria could be lying on the floor, hurt, so there was little we could do but go in and investigate.

"Um…you coming, Tan?"

"Yeah…" She snatched a quick breath. "But I'm warning you, Katrina, if we trip over another dead body I'm definitely not hanging around this time. You can ring 000. I'll be the one bolting back to the car and taking off like a Formula One driver."

"Hey," I assured her, "if there's a dead body in there, I'll beat you to the car."

A cold shiver shimmied up my spine, circled around into my chest and settled like a block of ice somewhere in the vicinity of my heart. Why the heck did Tanya have to mention dead bodies? As if it wasn't scary enough walking into an unfamiliar house in the dark at two in the morning, when the owner of the house was mysteriously not around, without adding a corpse to the mix. The only area I was familiar with was Gloria's lounge and the workroom at the end of the passageway. If I couldn't find Gloria, at least I could find the workroom, pick up Liz's dress, leave Gloria a note and then beat a hasty retreat.

Palms out, I groped blindly along the passage wall, stubbing my toe on what could have been a wooden box and colliding with a desk or a small table hard against the wall. There was a crash as something fell and hit the floor and I prayed it wasn't one of Gloria's valuable antiques. Why hadn't I checked out the whereabouts of all the light switches in the house when I had the chance during daylight? This was like waking up in the dark when sleepwalking and feeling around, wondering where the heck you were.

At last the never-ending passageway came to an abrupt end. I turned the handle of what I figured must be the workroom door and pushed it open. "Hey, Gloria! It's Kat. Are you in there?"

The darkness inside the room was absolute.

"Oof!" I grunted as Tanya bumped into me from behind, almost sending me onto my knees.

"Where's the freakin' light switch?"

"Feel along the wall," I told her. "The switch's gotta be here somewhere."

Tanya's hot breath, harsh in the eerie silence, gusted on the back of my neck as we stumbled further into the room. Invading my absent dressmaker's home hadn't been one of my better ideas. I reached back and grabbed for the bottom of Tanya's jacket–but she'd moved away. "Where are you?" The blackness seemed to close in around me. I was struggling to breathe. It was like the smothering darkness was sucking all the air from my lungs and if I didn't find either Tanya or the light switch in five seconds or less, I'd start screaming and choking and yanking at my hair and end up in a damp twisted heap of insanity on the floor.

"Ouch! That hurt!"

"What happened?" I whispered, abnormally pleased to hear Tanya's voice. But why was I whispering? "What happened?" I repeated, forcing the words to come out of my mouth at a normal pitch.

"Bumped into the corner of a table. I think."

"Well, you won't find the light switch over there."

"Okay, okay!"

Suddenly, a thin beam of light appeared from the direction I'd last heard Tanya's voice. "Oh, my, God, you're a genius, Tan," I said, relief running through me like a dose of salts. "Why didn't I think of using the torch on my phone?"

When Tanya's torch found the light switch high on the wall by the door, I beat her to the button and turned it on. Immediately the room was bathed in dazzling light. After the darkness the intense brightness made me blink.

"Well, well, well. Took you long enough." The voice, sing-song and high-pitched, came from behind us.

I spun around and felt my jaw drop. There was Gloria relaxing on a wooden chair, legs stretched out in front of her, head to one side, smiling at us. She'd been there all the time. But what made my jaw almost hit the floor was the shiny silver gun clamped in her right hand. I shook my head to clear the fog. And for some insane reason the thought flitted through my brain–geez, if I'd known my quiet introverted dressmaker was going to get this upset about altering Liz's dress, I'd have let my sister walk down the aisle wearing a hessian sack and Birkenstocks.

Tanya, face like chalk, opened her mouth to speak, but nothing came out.

"Gloria!" I croaked, still hoping this was a silly April fools' joke, in September. "What-what are you doing?"

Gloria tut-tutted like an old schoolmarm and shrugged her shoulders. "Look, I'm sorry, Kat, I quite like you, but when you and your Gran dropped your sister's dress off earlier today you saw everything."

"Everything?" I struggled to keep my voice from cracking. "What are you talking about?"

"The magazines and the glue and the scissors on my cutting-table. You even saw the special parchment paper in the notebook I used."

She'd lost me. "What magazines? What glue and scissors? Gloria, have you been working too hard? Why don't you put that gun away and I'll make you a nice cup of chamomile tea and we'll forget everything that's happened here tonight?"

"No can do." She raised her weapon higher and aimed it dead square at the middle of my forehead. I think I almost wet my pants as I stared into those two little black holes at the business end of her gun. "Shame really," she continued in a matter-of-fact tone. "See, I have nothing personally against you, or your friend. You detested Mary Parker as much as I did, but you had to go and play detective and spoil all my plans, didn't you?"

Oh, my God. When the Calendar Band started playing Here Comes the Bride on the sands of Semaphore in a little over an hour's time–there'd be no bride to walk down the aisle. I'd be a bloody corpse on Gloria's floor. A dead body for someone else to stumble over.

And what about Tanya? My Matron of Honor? There wouldn't be one of those at my wedding either. Oh yeah, and Liz would have to dress in her latest hippie clothes and be yelled at by Ma.

"Right. Down to business. You!" Gloria indicated Tanya with a wave of her gun. "Place your phone on the table and then move away from it."

Tanya flicked a wide-eyed 'oh shit!' expression in my direction and dropped her mobile onto the wooden table.

"Now, stand over there next to Kat. I'm sorry you had to find yourself in the middle of all this, Tanya, but you should have stayed home."

"But I–"

"Don't talk. Move!"

Afraid to move my head in case the mad woman with the gun blew it off, I slid my eyes sideways and watched Tanya, hyperventilating at every step as she marched stiff-legged across the room to stand beside me. I could smell the fear emanating from her–or was that me?

Still eyeing the two deadly black holes at the end of Gloria's gun, I figured I couldn't just stand there like a blob of cream cheese on a cracker and let Gloria shoot us. I had to do something. But what? Maybe I could kick the gun out of her hand. Or I could keep her talking, give myself time to work on a better plan. Deep inside, the rumblings of a panic attack stirred. Oh God. This wasn't happening. Okay. Keep calm. I straightened my shoulders. As I knew as much about kick boxing as I knew about conjugating Latin verbs, I'd keep her talking. "Why, Gloria?" I said, my voice little more than a whisper. "Why did you do it?"

The woman behind the gun narrowed her eyes at me. "Which why would you like me to answer first, Katrina? Why did I kill Mary? Why did I kill Peter? Or why do I have to kill you?"

"Um…" My throat, dry and cracked, closed over as I tried to force more words out. I swallowed in an attempt to suck up enough saliva to continue talking. Maybe if I could get Gloria to expand on all those whys, someone at home might realize we hadn't returned and send out a search party. "But you're a good person, Gloria. Why would you want to kill anyone?"

"See that dress over there?" she said indicating the gorgeous purple dress Gran had been admiring on the model earlier in the day. Earlier in the day when both Tanya and I weren't facing death by a fast-moving bullet. "Well, that dress is for the flashy woman-of-the-night who ended up marrying my fiancé. Yes, my fiancé. The man who Mary Parker tricked into becoming obsessed with degrading sexual acts." Her finger tensed on the trigger. I closed my eyes. Maybe talking wasn't such a good idea. "Mary Parker changed my once gentle, shy Adrian into a sex-fiend. Into a man who rates performances in the bedroom over moral values. A man who'd rather consort with fancy women who flash their assets like dirty washing." Her voice was holier-than-though pious, but I could hear the simmering fury behind the self-righteous speech. She narrowed her eyes at me. "And then, when Mary had him hooked and thoroughly perverted, she dumped him." Her entire face twisted into a mask of evil. "And of course, after that, I wasn't good enough in bed for Adrian anymore. So he broke off our engagement. And two weeks ago, he married Tawny Lightfeather, a brazen prostitute from a low-class brothel."

"But Gloria, your fiancé had choices too. Surely it was as much his fault as Mary's."

I may as well not have spoken for all the notice she took. By now Gloria's eyes were spinning with some inner fire. "How I hated Mary Parker. Wanted to spit in her face every time I saw her. But when she came around here a few nights ago, staggering drunk and taunting me for my inadequacies, I snapped. Decided the woman had to die. Okay, I knew I couldn't take Mary in a one-on-one fight, so I stole a couple of Jules' guns when I dropped by to pick up her bridesmaid dress for alterations, then I drove straight from Jules' house to Mary's and shot the bitch. Put a bullet right through those fake silicone implants and into her heart, bundled her into the boot of my car and as soon as it got dark, drove to the greyhound track. Yeah, I heaved Mary Parker up into the dumpster and left her there with all the other filthy rubbish. Exactly where she deserved to be."

Holy Toledo! Looking at Gloria's medium sized build it showed how a gut full of anger could turn even the most ordinary woman into a ball of strength and commitment.

"I know you had reason to hate Mary," put in Tanya who must have guessed at what I was doing. "But what about poor Peter? Why kill him?" She sounded indignant. I gave her a quick nudge. No need to get the madwoman all riled up. But she was on a roll. "What did Peter ever do to you, Gloria? Nothing, that's what. He was an inoffensive guy who loved his dogs and was just starting to move forward with his life when you took him out. Hey, the guy hated Mary as much as you did. He lost his family when she tricked him into her bed."

Gloria seemed to drift back down to earth as she shook her head and suddenly looked tired, much older than her forty-something years. "Yes, I admit, I was sorry about Peter. He was in love with Jules, you know." She sighed but the gun didn't move off target. "And of course when Jules was arrested he started to sniff around, wanting to prove she had nothing to do with Mary's murder, so I had to send him a warning– just like you–but he recognized the parchment paper I'd used and rung me, said if I didn't give myself up, he'd inform the police. What could I do? I had to kill him. Wasn't easy, but I hid behind the cupboard until he came into the kitchen and when he turned his back on me, I hit him over the head with his doorstop. Foolish man. I had no beef with Peter. If only he'd let it go, he'd still be alive." She shrugged, like it was everyone's fault, but hers. "And now you're doing the same thing."

"You can't just go around killing everyone who gets in your way,

Gloria," I said frantically trying to think up plan B. If we tried to run, Gloria would shoot us. If we stayed where we were, Gloria would shoot us. And I'd never get to say' I do' to Ben. He'd be so pissed off with me. I sighed, cast a quick glance across at Tanya and saw my own fear reflected in her eyes too. She was probably thinking about her daughter, Erin, who'd be left in the care of her useless ex-husband. A guy who couldn't hold down a job for longer than two days.

Gloria frowned. "Actually, I've decided not to shoot you – unless you try to escape."

"You're not?" For a moment I was so relieved, I forgot to breathe.

"Instead, I'll let you and Tanya crawl into the hundred-year-old cavity hidden under this floor." She must have noticed our horrified expressions because she smiled a thin smile that made my skin crawl. "This house isn't a century old for nothing. It has a history," she went on, still smiling. "I've discovered quite a few hidey holes since I bought it. All with macabre stories attached to them. But the one under this floor is perfect because it's just big enough for the two of you to snuggle up and die together."

"Nooo!" Tanya whispered, her eyes huge.

Icy shards of fear sliced through my intestines and I clenched my legs together as I fought against the panic that threatened to turn me into a pleading, crying mess at Gloria's feet. I had to stay strong. I had to wait for a chink in her amour. "Gloria, there's…there's no need for that," I croaked, cleared my throat and started again. "No need to do anything but tie us up and escape in your car. I saw your cases in the passageway. Don't shoot us–or bury us in a hole–just go!"

Gloria cocked her head to one side, thinking, and then shook her head slowly. "Sorry. Wouldn't work. I need to get well away from here before you're found. Although, to be honest, you'll need the luck of the Irish. That's the beauty of my hidey hole–it's both air-tight and sound-proof."

"No!" I took a step forward. No way was I going anywhere that was air-tight and sound-proof.

The two black holes at the end of her gun were in line with my head again and Gloria's eyes said she'd be just as happy to pull the trigger, if I took one more step in her direction. "Or I could shoot you both first and then dump you in the hole," she said. "It's your choice."

"Some choice."

"Well, this way, there's a tiny sliver of a chance you'll still be breathing if your friends find you within say…twenty minutes. But if I shoot you first, you're already dead." She shrugged and then indicated Tanya with her gun. "You, help Kat pull the rug away from under your feet and then roll it up neatly so I can replace it before I leave."

As Tanya and I heaved the thick red and black patterned rug into a long cylindrical roll, all I could see underneath was the gray cement floor. What now? Her gun still trained on us, Gloria stood up and took two steps backward, then reached up and pressed one of what appeared to be a row of oak-colored wooden cornices placed at eye-level along the wall.

Slowly, soundlessly, a section of the floor slid open under our feet.

"Hey!" I yelped as both Tanya and I were forced to scramble backward.

Regaining my balance, I peered down into the cement-lined rectangular hole in the floor. This couldn't be happening. It had to be a nightmare. Today was supposed to be the happiest day of my life. I was due to get married–not die. Dread, like a heavy stone, crept along my arms and legs, pinning me to the spot. I closed my eyes and then looked again. The hole was barely big enough for two people to lie down, side by side.

That's when my stomach did a sickening double hitch and the wine and orange juice I'd consumed earlier threatened to hurl. And when I tried to scream, my breath caught in my throat and all that came out was a gasping, gurgling wheeze.

If Tanya and I were forced to lie down in that shallow cavity and Gloria pressed the button for the floor to slide back into place–we'd be buried alive.

19

Long seconds passed as Tanya and I stared down into the dark dingy hole at our feet. A shallow hole under the cement. A grave for two. My skin, cold and clammy, crawled at the horror of it. Like little biting insects burrowing through my skin and gnawing on my entrails.

I couldn't die in there. No one deserved to die like that.

So why was I waiting for a chink in her armor, to pounce? Do something!

"Okay, in you go, girls. Hop to it."

I lifted my head and gaped at her. Was she serious? Gloria, the crazy woman waving a gun, acted and spoke as though she was a brisk tour guide in charge of a group and Tanya and I were the last two passengers, dilly dallying and taking far too long to board the tour bus.

Instead of a burial chamber.

"I know it's not ideal, but this way is much easier for me," Gloria explained in what she probably thought was a rational tone. "I don't want to shoot you–too much blood to clean up before I leave." She shrugged one shoulder and her unnerving smile reminded me of a character from a Steven King thriller. The one where the deranged fan of some author smiled while chopping off his leg so he couldn't leave.

When neither of us moved, Gloria steadied her gun and scowled. "Unless you refuse to cooperate, of course."

Cooperate? She had to be joking. No way was I stepping into that hole–I'd rather be shot. At least I'd die quickly instead of slowly running out of air in a space no bigger than a coffin. And I could see by Tanya's set jaw that she'd rather take a chance and die by bullet too. In fact, Tanya, always much braver than me, had folded her arms and stood, legs apart, glaring at Gloria. Indicating she was going nowhere.

"Oh, come on, now. It won't be too bad. You'll have enough air for at least…twenty minutes. And cleaning up blood is so messy and time-consuming. My plane leaves for to the States in a couple of hours and I have to be at the airport an hour before departure." She glanced at her watch and then shook her head at us like an exasperated parent. "Okay, last chance. Get in there or I'll shoot you right where you're standing."

From the corner of my eye I caught a quick flash of something blue–cerulean blue–on the other side of the open workroom door. And then it was gone. Heard a soft footstep – followed by silence. My imagination? Wishful thinking? Maybe not, as Gloria's eyes flicked momentarily in that direction too.

Providing the chink in her armor I'd been waiting for.

With no time to contemplate the excruciating pain of a lead-tipped bullet ripping through flesh and bone from a mere distance of three feet, and that I'd never see Ben or my dogs again, I launched myself at Gloria. I heard the crack of a bullet as it hissed past my head and watched her finger tighten on the trigger for a replay.

It was like watching a movie in slow motion. Gloria's eyes widened. Her mouth twisted in a snarl. Her trigger finger tensed again. But before she could finish the action and fire, a shot rang out from the other side of the room. In mid-air, I watched Gloria's gun fly from her hand, spin high in the air, hit the brightly painted yellow wall and then bounce down into the open hole at her feet.

My body slammed into Gloria's chest and took her backwards, spitting and screaming and snarling like a fox caught in a trap, while Tanya grabbed hold of her legs and hung on with terrier-like tenacity. Fighting to keep Gloria from throwing us both off, I lifted my head, desperate for more people-power and took in Jules, face a mask of concentration, still in a bent-knee stance, just inside the doorway. It was Jules who'd shot the gun from Gloria's hand. My friend, Jules Cassidy, gorgeous in her cerulean blue bridesmaid's dress, wasn't an Australian Target Shooting champion for nothing.

"Could do with some help here…" I let out a grunt as one of Gloria's fists smacked into the side of my head. "Like now!"

Immediately Jules straightened and hurried forward, her gun aimed at Gloria. With her perfect make-up, beautiful blue bridesmaid dress and long fair hair swinging in soft waves down her back, you wouldn't believe how deadly Jules could be with a gun. But the frown etched on her forehead and the no-nonsense glint in her eyes belied her soft looks.

Thunder appeared in the doorway, mobile phone attached to her ear and a pair of handcuffs–not the soft fluffy variety found in Tanya's shop–swinging from her other hand. She finished her conversation and shoved the phone in her pocket. "Stay down! Police!" she yelled at Gloria as she strode across the room, the soft taffeta of her midi-length emerald green dress shushing with each step and the high heels on her strappy black sandals clicking on the cement. I blinked. Out of her black leather, Scuzz's biker half-sister actually looked kinda cute. Although the handcuffs and the steely cop face definitely took the edge off her cuteness. "The police are on their way, Gloria," she said eying the wrestling match on the floor, so stop with all that useless struggling or I'll instruct my deputy here to shoot the dirt out from under your fingernails. She is normally an excellent shot, but due to the fact that you've made her really, really mad, first by framing her for murder and then by threatening to kill her friends, you may also lose a couple of fingers along with the dirt."

"Deputy?" Jules lifted one eyebrow and the slightest trace of a grin touched her lips. "Okay, you can get off now," she said to Tanya and me. "I've got her in my sights. The piece of slime only has to move a muscle and her finger nails are history."

I clambered to my feet, discovered my legs had mysteriously metamorphosed into bendy stretchy licorice sticks and lurched in the direction of the nearest chair. I needed a moment. Not every day does a person have a murderous dressmaker bent on disrupting their wedding day by ensuring the bride was too dead to attend.

Thunder, handcuffs at the ready, blinked down at Tanya who still held Gloria's legs in a death-grip. "Um…Tan? You okay down there? Just that's it's a bit difficult to get these babies around the offender's wrists with you parked on top of her."

Eying Gloria like the insidious reptile she was, Tanya cautiously stood up and took a step away. "Okay, she's all yours…but can I just kick her in the ribs first?"

Thunder shook her head. "Only if she tries to get up without permission."

The expression on Tanya's face as she glared down at the woman on the floor obviously said, please get up, please get up! But all the fight had gone out of Gloria. She was now curled into a fetal ball, mumbling to herself.

Jules kept her gun on Gloria until Thunder finished restraining her, then stepped down into the floor cavity–our almost grave. "So" she said, her voice scarily icy. "This is where she intended leaving you?" When I nodded she raised narrowed eyes to Thunder. "Like, couldn't we just roll Gloria in here and close it up–you know, just for a few minutes? Seems a shame not to give it a test run."

Thunder hauled Gloria to her feet and shook her head. "Maybe I'd better escort our prisoner out onto the footpath and wait there. Think I can hear the sound of police sirens, anyway."

"Pity," said Jules winking as she linked arms with Tanya and me. "Sometimes it's no fun at all being a law-abiding citizen."

With a last quick glance over my shoulder at that chilling gray cement hole in the floor where Tanya and I had come close to breathing our last, I shivered.

"No fun at all," I agreed.

20

THE SKY MET THE OCEAN IN A KALEIDOSCOPE of golds and browns and reds against the darker mauves and purples of the sea. An artist's palette gone large. It was daybreak and the heels of my white satin shoes sunk in the heavy sand as I hopped nervously from one foot to the other in a makeshift, tent-like room. I was squashed in with my two bridesmaids, my matron of honor, my hyped-up flower girl and the four dogs who were accompanying us down the aisle. Hidden from my wedding guests who were still chattering and claiming seats on either side of the long grass mat that led to the wedding-celebrant, we were waiting for the first notes of The Wedding March.

I tugged my veil over my face and then ran a hand down the front of my dress to smooth the lace. The dress both my mother and grandmother had worn at their own wedding. It fitted perfectly, thanks to the dressmaker who'd worked so hard cutting, sewing and fitting the dresses for my wedding day and then promptly decided to stop me from attending– in the worst possible way.

"Where's that deadbeat uncle of yours?" Tanya, her nose through a slit in the tent flap, was busy checking proceedings. "Can't see him anywhere." Surprisingly, Tanya had pulled up quite chirpy after our run-in with Gloria, the murderous dressmaker. However, my legs were still a bit marshmallow-like after our ordeal. "Hoo hoo! I can't believe my eyes," Tanya yelped. "Here's Scuzz! Well, I think it's Scuzz."

The tent flap opened and a seven-foot giant appeared. Seven feet of mean muscle. Of tattoo-covered biker–but with not a shred of shiny black leather or a red bandanna in sight. Instead, he sported a made-to-measure elegant tuxedo, complete with bow tie and perfectly groomed ginger beard. My mouth opened wide enough to swallow an entire shark. "Scuzz? Is that you?"

The big man smiled through his beard and when he spoke his voice was hushed, almost reverent. "Katrina, my darling girl, you look beautiful. Absolutely beautiful."

It took a moment to find my voice which had somehow got tangled up with the lump in my throat. "Thanks, Scuzz. And you look pretty crash hot yourself." And he did. From his shiny black loafers to his expertly tied black bow tie, Theodore Samuel Parkington the Third, looked as far from a Harley-riding street-cred biker as a dirty dish cloth to a finely creased satin handkerchief.

My sister cocked her head to the side and gave him a top to toe inspection before standing on tiptoe and straightening his bow tie. "As lickably gorgeous as you look, big boy, you shouldn't be in this tent. It's for the wedding party only."

"Lickably gorgeous?" he repeated, a huge grin spreading across his face as he raised one of his ginger eyebrows at her.

Liz punched him on the arm. "Don't get too bigheaded there, Theodore. You may be tongue- licking material, but I'm a happily married woman." She patted her baby bump as though to prove it. "And you still haven't told us what you're doing in here."

Scuzz's eyes rested on me and for a moment he looked vulnerable, like a little boy in trouble. "Unfortunately," he said, drawing out the word. "Your Uncle Tony isn't here."

Oh, god, what else could go wrong?

"Long story short–he arrived falling-down drunk so your Ma sent him home with a flea in his ear."

"How am I supposed to get married without a father-of-the-bride?"

Scuzz tugged nervously at his beard. "Well…I'm his replacement. I mean, if that's acceptable to you, Katrina."

I let out a sigh and reached for his hand which was still pulling at his beard, gave it a reassuring squeeze. "Scuzz, I'm honored. Other than my Dad, you're the person I would most want to lead me down the aisle.

Okay?" When his huge hand wrapped around mine and squeezed back, a tear threatened my mascara. I dabbed at it with one finger and gently wiped it away.

"Hey," Liz broke in, eyes alight with mischief. "What sort of flea did Ma put in Uncle Tony's ear?"

"Let's just say a flea that bit his ear so hard he'll be without hearing for at least a week."

"Okay, guys, let's get this show on the road," said Tanya as the first notes of Here Comes the Bride swept across the early morning beach front. She lifted the tent flap and gave Erin a small push in the back before she and Lofty stepped out onto the grass matting. Jules and Liz shortened Lucky and Yolo's leads and fell in behind Tanya.

"Last chance, Katrina," Scuzz whispered from the corner of his mouth as he hooked onto my arm with his massive paw and ushered me out of the tent and onto the grass matting. "Last chance to dump the cowboy and marry me."

I poked him in the ribs as we began our step-together-step-together march down the aisle. "Behave yourself, Scuzz," I whispered back and then grinned up at him, not wanting to deflate his ego. "Okay, I admit you do send my lady bits into orbit at times–but the one I love with all my heart is standing down there, waiting for me."

"Only reason I gave up trying." He shrugged and then smiled and sent me a mischievous wink. "But nice to know the effect I have on your lady bits."

In time to the music, we continued the long walk down the aisle. On both sides, the white plastic chairs held friends and relatives, all smiling at me. There was D. I. Adams, looking even more like Colombo in his dog-eared long coat and sporting a ten o'clock shadow. He gave me a thumbs up and a tired grin. Thanks to him, I'd arrived only ten minutes late for my wedding as he'd provided a police escort from Gloria's house to mine and from my house to Semaphore beach.

But the only person I had eyes for was waiting for me at the end of the aisle. Benjamin Taylor. My Ben, looking cool in a silver-gray suit, a huge smile plastered on his face, his eyes never leaving me.

The moment I arrived, Ben's hand reached for mine. I fitted my hand into his and grinned up at him. His returning smile was tentative and the hand I was holding icy cold. Close now, I could see how pale Ben looked and grimaced. I guess when your bride is not only ten minutes late for her wedding but also arrives with a police escort, sirens wailing, it might have that effect on a guy.

Delta, our witchy celebrant, blinked several times as though she'd been far, far away in a pleasant land where unicorns roamed and fairies spread happiness like glitter. "Friends, we have been invited here today, at the rising of the sun, to share with Benjamin and Katrina a very important moment in their lives…"

"You okay, babe?" Ben whispered from the side of his mouth.

"Yeah. Sure. Never better."

A small frown wrinkled his forehead. "But what's with the police cars?" He shook his head and for one ugly moment I thought he was going to tut-tut at me. "You're not in trouble again, are you?"

My smile faded. "What do you mean? Again!"

He quickly shook his head. "I mean… I was worried about you, babe."

I glanced at Delta who'd stopped spouting wedding ceremony talk and stood, arms folded, glowering at us. "Um, not now, Ben," I whispered, squeezing his fingers in a death grip to warn him. "I'll fill you in later."

Delta let out a small growl–just a reminder as to what she was capable of doing with her witchy powers, when annoyed. "You two quite finished?"

"Yes, of course. Sorry."

She drew herself up to her full height of five foot nothing, tossed her long golden hair off her shoulders, and started again. "Friends, we have been invited here today, at the rising of the sun, to share with Katrina and Benjamin, a very important moment in their lives. The joining of two hearts. In the years they have been together, their love and understanding of each other has grown and matured and now they have decided to live their lives together as husband and wife…"

The whole time Delta said her thing, I smiled up at Ben, argument forgotten, my heart full of love. Hey, he was worried about me–not trying to boss me. And instead of lying under a cement floor breathing my last, I was here on the beach with family and friends, marrying the guy I'd fallen in love with the first time I saw him at the track, bent over, and stuffing dog poo into black plastic bags.

"Benjamin," Delta turned to Ben. "Do you take Katrina to be your lawfully wedded wife? To love and to cherish and to always be there for her on the bad days as well as the good, until the day you die?"

"I sure do. And I'll even be there for her when she's off sleuthing instead of at home nuking a frozen box for our dinner."

There was a loud hoot from the crowd.

"And you, Katrina, do you take this man to be your lawfully wedded husband to love and to cherish and to–"

"I do. I do. I do." I broke in before she could finish. I just loved saying those two words. I lifted my veil and gazed at Ben's gorgeous familiar face, the face I wanted to see lying on the pillow beside me every morning when I woke up, for the rest of my life.

He gazed down at my lips and his eyes grew hot. His head crept closer, and then his lips, smoldering hot, met mine. I dropped my bouquet of white freesias in the sand and slid both arms up around his neck. It felt like coming home.

"Not yet!" squawked Delta and I heard her stamp her foot but was too busy tasting Ben's mouth to care. She could have evoked bolts of lightning from the sky and I still wouldn't care. "It's the ring ceremony next."

Ben's tongue slid inside my mouth.

"No, no, no! We have to do the Exchange of rings and the Pronouncement before you can do that, guys," she said and it sounded like she was jumping up and down. "It's not kissy time yet."

Ben shifted his head slightly to get a better angle on my lips. His hand strayed down my back. And when his tongue began simulating sex and his hand, warm on my ass, lifted me a little higher, I could feel my lady bits roaring with delight. Oh God, how I loved this guy.

From the corner of my eye I saw Delta throw her hands in the air and shake her head. "Oh bugger," she growled. "I now pronounce you man and wife."

Dear Readers

Leashed is the fourth book in my Kat McKinley greyhound mysteries. These books have been so much fun to write. If you enjoyed reading about Kat and her zany friends and loveable greyhounds, please pop over to Amazon and leave an honest review. Reviews are so helpful to authors. In fact, they are part of what keeps us writing – knowing our readers enjoy our books.

Also, if you'd like to catch up with me on Facebook go to: https://www.facebook.com/JuneWhyteBooks.

Or to check out my website go here: www.junewhytebooks.com.

Thank you,

June Whyte